THE BOXCAR CHILDREN®

Fully Illustrated Edition

The Boxcar Children Mysteries

The Boxcar Children
Surprise Island
The Yellow House Mystery
Mystery Ranch
Mike's Mystery
Blue Bay Mystery
The Woodshed Mystery
The Lighthouse Mystery
Mountain Top Mystery
Schoolhouse Mystery
Caboose Mystery
Houseboat Mystery
Snowbound Mystery
Tree House Mystery
Bicycle Mystery
Mystery in the Sand
Mystery Behind the Wall
Bus Station Mystery
Benny Uncovers a Mystery
The Haunted Cabin Mystery
The Deserted Library Mystery
The Animal Shelter Mystery
The Old Motel Mystery
The Mystery of the Hidden Painting
The Amusement Park Mystery
The Mystery of the Mixed-Up Zoo
The Camp-Out Mystery
The Mystery Girl
The Mystery Cruise
The Disappearing Friend Mystery
The Mystery of the Singing Ghost
The Mystery in the Snow
The Pizza Mystery
The Mystery Horse
The Mystery at the Dog Show
The Castle Mystery
The Mystery of the Lost Village
The Mystery on the Ice
The Mystery of the Purple Pool
The Ghost Ship Mystery
The Mystery in Washington, DC
The Canoe Trip Mystery
The Mystery of the Hidden Beach
The Mystery of the Missing Cat
The Mystery at Snowflake Inn
The Mystery on Stage
The Dinosaur Mystery
The Mystery of the Stolen Music
The Mystery at the Ball Park
The Chocolate Sundae Mystery
The Mystery of the Hot Air Balloon
The Mystery Bookstore
The Pilgrim Village Mystery
The Mystery of the Stolen Boxcar
The Mystery in the Cave
The Mystery on the Train
The Mystery at the Fair
The Mystery of the Lost Mine

The Guide Dog Mystery
The Hurricane Mystery
The Pet Shop Mystery
The Mystery of the Secret Message
The Firehouse Mystery
The Mystery in San Francisco
The Niagara Falls Mystery
The Mystery at the Alamo
The Outer Space Mystery
The Soccer Mystery
The Mystery in the Old Attic
The Growling Bear Mystery
The Mystery of the Lake Monster
The Mystery at Peacock Hall
The Windy City Mystery
The Black Pearl Mystery
The Cereal Box Mystery
The Panther Mystery
The Mystery of the Queen's Jewels
The Stolen Sword Mystery
The Basketball Mystery
The Movie Star Mystery
The Mystery of the Pirate's Map
The Ghost Town Mystery
The Mystery of the Black Raven
The Mystery in the Mall
The Mystery in New York
The Gymnastics Mystery
The Poison Frog Mystery
The Mystery of the Empty Safe
The Home Run Mystery
The Great Bicycle Race Mystery
The Mystery of the Wild Ponies
The Mystery in the Computer Game
The Honeybee Mystery
The Mystery at the Crooked House
The Hockey Mystery
The Mystery of the Midnight Dog
The Mystery of the Screech Owl
The Summer Camp Mystery
The Copycat Mystery
The Haunted Clock Tower Mystery
The Mystery of the Tiger's Eye
The Disappearing Staircase Mystery
The Mystery on Blizzard Mountain
The Mystery of the Spider's Clue
The Candy Factory Mystery
The Mystery of the Mummy's Curse
The Mystery of the Star Ruby
The Stuffed Bear Mystery
The Mystery of Alligator Swamp
The Mystery at Skeleton Point
The Tattletale Mystery
The Comic Book Mystery
The Great Shark Mystery
The Ice Cream Mystery
The Midnight Mystery
The Mystery in the Fortune Cookie

The Black Widow Spider Mystery
The Radio Mystery
The Mystery of the Runaway Ghost
The Finders Keepers Mystery
The Mystery of the Haunted Boxcar
The Clue in the Corn Maze
The Ghost of the Chattering Bones
The Sword of the Silver Knight
The Game Store Mystery
The Mystery of the Orphan Train
The Vanishing Passenger
The Giant Yo-Yo Mystery
The Creature in Ogopogo Lake
The Rock 'n' Roll Mystery
The Secret of the Mask
The Seattle Puzzle
The Ghost in the First Row
The Box That Watch Found
A Horse Named Dragon
The Great Detective Race
The Ghost at the Drive-In Movie
The Mystery of the Traveling Tomatoes
The Spy Game
The Dog-Gone Mystery
The Vampire Mystery
Superstar Watch
The Spy in the Bleachers
The Amazing Mystery Show
The Pumpkin Head Mystery
The Cupcake Caper
The Clue in the Recycling Bin
Monkey Trouble
The Zombie Project
The Great Turkey Heist
The Garden Thief
The Boardwalk Mystery
The Mystery of the Fallen Treasure
The Return of the Graveyard Ghost
The Mystery of the Stolen Snowboard
The Mystery of the Wild West Bandit
The Mystery of the Soccer Snitch
The Mystery of the Grinning Gargoyle
The Mystery of the Missing Pop Idol
The Mystery of the Stolen Dinosaur Bones
The Mystery at the Calgary Stampede
The Sleepy Hollow Mystery
The Legend of the Irish Castle
The Celebrity Cat Caper
Hidden in the Haunted School
The Election Day Dilemma
Journey on a Runaway Train
The Clue in the Papyrus Scroll
The Detour of the Elephants
The Shackleton Sabotage
The Khipu and the Final Key
The Doughnut Whodunit
The Robot Ransom

THE BOXCAR CHILDREN®

Fully Illustrated Edition

by Gertrude Chandler Warner

Illustrated by Anne Yvonne Gilbert
and Gretchen Ellen Powers

Albert Whitman & Company
Chicago, Illinois

Copyright © 2017 by Albert Whitman & Company
Published in 2017 by Albert Whitman & Company

ISBN 978-0-8075-0925-8

THE BOXCAR CHILDREN® is a registered
trademark of Albert Whitman & Company.

Printed in the United States of America
10 9 8 7 6 5 4 3 2 1 LB 22 21 20 19 18 17

Cover art copyright © 2017 by Anne Yvonne Gilbert
Interior illustrations copyright © 2017 by Gretchen Ellen Powers
Design by Ellen Kokontis

Visit the Boxcar Children online at www.boxcarchildren.com.
For more information about Albert Whitman & Company,
visit our website at www.albertwhitman.com.

Contents

Chapter 1

The Four Hungry Children

ONE WARM NIGHT four children stood in front of a bakery. No one knew them. No one knew where they had come from.

The baker's wife saw them first, as they stood looking in at the window of her store. The little boy was looking at the cakes, the big boy was looking at the loaves of bread, and the two girls were looking at the cookies.

Now the baker's wife did not like children. She did not like boys at all. So she came to the front of the bakery and listened, looking very cross.

"The cake is good, Jessie," the little boy said. He was about five years old.

"Yes, Benny," said the big girl. "But bread is better for you. Isn't it, Henry?"

1

"Oh yes," said Henry. "We must have some bread, and cake is not good for Benny and Violet."

"I like bread best, anyway," said Violet. She was about ten years old, and she had pretty brown hair and brown eyes.

"That is just like you, Violet," said Henry, smiling at her. "Let's go into the bakery. Maybe they will let us stay here for the night."

The baker's wife looked at them as they came in.

"I want three loaves of bread, please," said Jessie.

She smiled politely at the woman, but the woman did not smile. She looked at Henry as he put his hand in his pocket for the money. She looked cross, but she sold him the bread.

Jessie was looking around too, and she saw a long red bench under each window of the bakery. The benches had flat red pillows on them.

"Will you let us stay here for the night?" Jessie asked. "We could sleep on those benches, and tomorrow we would help you wash the dishes and do things for you."

Now the woman liked this. She did not like to wash

dishes very well. She would like to have a big boy to help her with her work.

"Where are your father and mother?" she asked.

"They are dead," said Henry.

"We have a grandfather in Greenfield, but we don't like him," said Benny.

Jessie put her hand over the little boy's mouth before he could say more.

"Oh, Benny, keep still!" she said.

"Why don't you like your grandfather?" asked the woman.

"He is our father's father, and he didn't like our mother," said Henry. "So we don't think he would like us. We are afraid he would be mean to us."

"Did you ever see him?" asked the woman.

"No," answered Henry.

"Then why do you think he would be mean to you?" asked the woman.

"Well, he never came to see us," said Henry. "He doesn't like us at all."

"Where did you live before you came here?" asked the woman.

But not one of the four children would tell her.

"We'll get along all right," said Jessie. "We want to stay here for only one night."

"You may stay here tonight," said the woman at last. "And tomorrow we'll see what we can do."

Henry thanked her politely.

"We are all pretty tired and hungry," he said.

The children sat down on the floor. Henry cut one of the loaves of bread into four pieces with his knife, and the children began to eat.

"Delicious!" said Henry.

"Well, I never!" said the woman.

She went into the next room and shut the door.

"I'm glad she is gone," remarked Benny, eating. "She doesn't like us."

"Sh, Benny!" said Jessie. "She is good to let us sleep here."

After supper the children lay down on their red benches, and Violet and Benny soon went to sleep.

But Jessie and Henry could hear the woman talking to the baker.

She said, "I'll keep the three older children. They can help me. But the little boy must go to the Children's Home. He is too little. I cannot take care of him."

The baker answered, "Very well. Tomorrow I'll take the little boy to the Children's Home. We'll keep the others for a while, but we must make them tell us who their grandfather is."

Jessie and Henry waited until the baker and his wife had gone to bed. Then they sat up in the dark.

"Oh, Henry!" whispered Jessie. "Let's run away from here!"

"Yes, indeed," said Henry. "We'll never let Benny go to a Children's Home. Never, never! We must be far away by morning, or they will find us. But we must not leave any of our things here."

Jessie sat still, thinking.

"Our clothes and a cake of soap and towels are in the big laundry bag," she said. "Violet has her little workbag. And we have two loaves of bread left. Have you your knife and the money?"

"Yes," said Henry. "I have almost four dollars."

"You must carry Benny," said Jessie. "He will cry if we wake him up. But I'll wake Violet.

"Sh, Violet! Come! We are going to run away again. If we don't run away, the baker will take Benny to a Children's Home in the morning."

The little girl woke up at once. She sat up and rolled off the bench. She did not make any noise.

"What shall I do?" she whispered softly.

"Carry this," said Jessie. She gave her the workbag.

Jessie put the two loaves of bread into the laundry bag, and then she looked around the room.

"All right," she said to Henry. "Take Benny now."

Henry took Benny in his arms and carried him to the door of the bakery. Jessie took the laundry bag and opened the door very softly. All the children went out quietly. They did not say a word. Jessie shut the door, and then they all listened. Everything was very quiet. So the four children went down the street.

Chapter 2

Night Is Turned into Day

SOON THE CHILDREN left the town and came to a road. The big yellow moon was out, and they could see the road very well.

"We must walk fast," said Henry. "I hope the baker and his wife don't wake up and find us gone."

They walked down the road as fast as they could.

"How far can you carry Benny?" asked Violet.

"Oh, I can carry him a long way," replied Henry.

But Jessie said, "I think we could go faster if we woke him up now. We could take his hands and help him along."

Henry stopped and put Benny down.

"Come, Benny," he said. "You must wake up and walk now."

"Go away!" said Benny.

"Let me try," said Violet. "Now, Benny, you can play

that you are a little brown bear and are running away to find a nice warm bed. Henry and Jessie will help you, and we'll find a bed."

Benny liked being a little brown bear, and so he woke up and opened his eyes. Henry and Jessie took his hands, and they all went on again.

They passed some farmhouses, but the houses were dark and quiet. The children did not see anyone. They walked and walked for a long time. Then the red sun began to come up.

"We must find a place to sleep," said Jessie. "I am so tired."

Little Benny was asleep, and Henry was carrying him again. The other children began to look for a place.

At last Violet said, "Look over there." She was pointing at a big haystack in a field near a farmhouse.

"A fine place, Violet," said Henry. "See what a big haystack it is!"

They ran across the field toward the farmhouse. They jumped over a brook, and then they came to the haystack.

Henry was still carrying Benny.

Jessie began to make a nest in the haystack for Benny, and when they put him into it, he went to sleep again at once. The other children also made nests.

"Good night!" said Henry, laughing.

"It is 'good morning' I should think," replied Jessie. "We sleep in the day, and we walk all night. When it is night again, we'll wake up and walk some more."

The children were so tired that they went right to sleep. They slept all day, and it was night again when they woke up.

Benny said at once, "Oh, Jessie, I'm hungry. I want something to eat."

"Good old Benny," said Henry. "We'll have supper."

Jessie took out a loaf of bread and cut it into four pieces. It was soon gone.

"I want some water," begged Benny.

"Not now," said Henry. "You may have some water when it gets dark. There is a pump near the farmhouse. But if we leave the haystack now, someone will see us."

When it was dark, the children came out of the haystack and went quietly toward the farmhouse, which was dark and still. Nearby was a pump, and Henry pumped water as quietly as he could. He did not even wake up the hens and chickens.

"I want a cup," said Benny.

"No, Benny," whispered Henry. "You will have to put your mouth right in the water. You can play you are a horse."

This pleased Benny. Henry pumped and pumped, and at last Benny had all the water he wanted. The water was cold and sweet, and all the children drank. Then they ran across the field toward the road.

"If we hear anyone," said Jessie, "we must hide behind the bushes."

Just as she said this, the children heard a horse and cart coming up the road.

"Keep very still, Benny!" whispered Henry. "Don't say a word."

The children got behind the bushes as fast as they could, for they did not have much time to hide. The horse came nearer and nearer and began to walk up the hill toward them. Then the children could hear a man talking. It was the baker!

"I wonder where those children went," he said. "I don't think they could walk as far as Silver City. If we don't find them in Greenfield, we'll go home."

"Yes," answered his wife. "I do not want to find them, anyway. I don't like children, but we must try a little while longer. We will look for them in Greenfield, and that's all."

The children watched until the horse and cart had gone down the road. Then they came out from behind the bushes and looked at each other.

"My, I am glad those people did not see us!" said Henry. "You were a good boy, Benny, to keep still.

"We'll not go to Greenfield."

"I wonder how far it is to Silver City," said Jessie.

The children were very happy as they walked along the road. They knew that the baker would not find them. They walked until two o'clock in the morning, and then they came to some signs by the side of the road.

The moon came out from behind the clouds, and Henry could read the signs.

"One sign says that Greenfield is this way," he said. "The other sign points to Silver City. We don't want to go to Greenfield. Let's take this other road to Silver City."

They walked for a long time, but they did not see anyone.

"Not many people come this way, I guess," said Henry. "But that is all the better."

"Listen!" said Benny suddenly. "I hear something."

"Listen!" said Violet.

The children stood still and listened, and they could hear water running.

"I want a drink of water, Henry!" said Benny.

"Well, let's go on," said Henry, "and see where the water is. I'd like a drink too."

Soon the children saw a drinking fountain by the side of the road.

"Oh, what a fine fountain this is!" said Henry, running toward it. "See the place for people to drink up high,

15

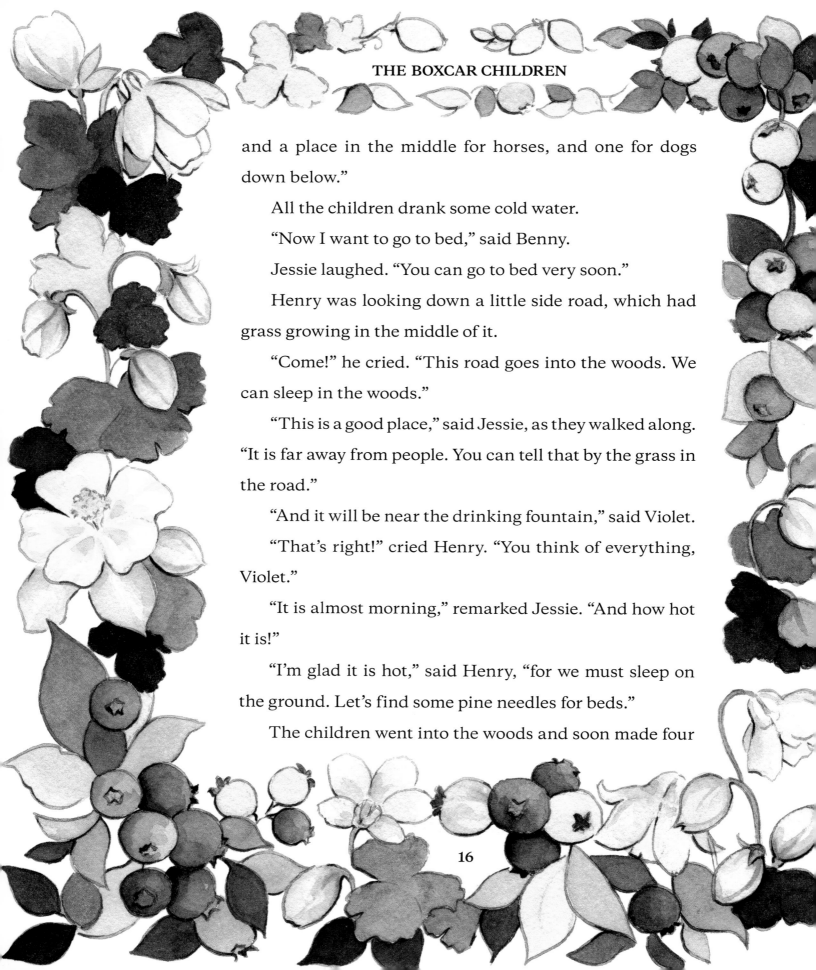

and a place in the middle for horses, and one for dogs down below."

All the children drank some cold water.

"Now I want to go to bed," said Benny.

Jessie laughed. "You can go to bed very soon."

Henry was looking down a little side road, which had grass growing in the middle of it.

"Come!" he cried. "This road goes into the woods. We can sleep in the woods."

"This is a good place," said Jessie, as they walked along. "It is far away from people. You can tell that by the grass in the road."

"And it will be near the drinking fountain," said Violet.

"That's right!" cried Henry. "You think of everything, Violet."

"It is almost morning," remarked Jessie. "And how hot it is!"

"I'm glad it is hot," said Henry, "for we must sleep on the ground. Let's find some pine needles for beds."

The children went into the woods and soon made four

beds of pine needles.

"I hope it's not going to rain," said Jessie, as she lay down.

Then she looked up at the sky.

"It looks like rain, for the moon has gone behind the clouds."

She shut her eyes and did not open them again for a long time.

More clouds rolled across the sky, and the wind began to blow. There was lightning also, and thunder, but the children did not hear it. They were all fast asleep.

Chapter 3

A New Home in the Woods

AT LAST JESSIE opened her eyes. It was morning, but the sun was covered by clouds. She sat up and looked all around her, and then she looked at the sky. It seemed like night, for it was very dark. Suddenly it began to thunder, and she saw that it was really going to rain.

"What shall we do? Where shall we go?" thought Jessie.

The wind was blowing more and more clouds across the sky, and the lightning was very near.

She walked a little way into the woods, looking for a place to go out of the rain.

"Where shall we go?" she thought again.

Then she saw something ahead of her in the woods. It was an old boxcar.

"What a good house that will be in the rain!" she thought.

She ran over to the boxcar. There was no engine, and the track was old and rusty. It was covered with grass and bushes because it had not been used for a long time.

"It *is* a boxcar," Jessie said. "We can get into it and stay until it stops raining."

She ran back as fast as she could to the other children. The sky was black, and the wind was blowing very hard.

"Hurry! Hurry!" cried Jessie. "I have found a good place! Hurry as fast as you can!"

Henry took Benny's hand, and they all ran through the woods after Jessie.

"It's beginning to rain!" cried Henry.

"We'll soon be there," Jessie shouted back. "It is not far. When we get there, you must help me open the door. It is heavy."

The stump of a big tree stood under the door of the boxcar and was just right for a step. Jessie and Henry jumped up on the old dead stump and rolled back the heavy door of the car. Henry looked in.

"There is nothing in here," he said. "Come, Benny.

We'll help you up."

Violet went in next, and, last of all, Jessie and Henry climbed in.

They were just in time. How the wind did blow! They rolled the door shut, and then it really began to rain. Oh, how it did rain! It just rained and rained. The children could hear it on the top of the boxcar, but no rain came in.

"What a good place this is!" said Violet. "It is just like a warm little house with one room."

After a while the rain and lightning and thunder stopped, and the wind did not blow so hard. Then Henry opened the door and looked out. All the children looked out into the woods. The sun was shining, but some water still fell from the trees. In front of the boxcar a pretty little brook ran over the rocks, with a waterfall in it.

"What a beautiful place!" said Violet.

"Henry!" cried Jessie. "Let's live here!"

"Live here?" asked Henry.

"Yes! Why not?" said Jessie. "This boxcar is a fine little house. It is dry and warm in the rain."

"We could wash in the brook," said Violet.

"Please, Henry," begged Jessie. "We could have the nicest little home here, and we could find some dishes, and make four beds and a table, and maybe chairs!"

"No," said Benny. "I don't want to live here, Jessie."

"Oh dear, why not, Benny?" asked Jessie.

"I'm afraid the engine will come and take us away," answered Benny.

Henry and Jessie laughed. "Oh no, Benny," said Henry. "The engine will never take this car away. It is an old, old car, and grass and bushes are growing all over the track."

"Then doesn't the engine use this track anymore?" asked Benny.

"No, indeed," said Henry. He was beginning to want to live in the boxcar too.

"We'll stay here today, anyway,"

"Then can I have my dinner here?" asked Benny.

"Yes, you shall have dinner now," said Henry.

So Jessie took out the last loaf of bread and cut it into four pieces, but it was very dry. Benny ate the bread, but soon he began to cry.

"I want some milk too, Jessie," he begged.

"He ought to have milk," said Henry. "I'll go to the next town and get some."

But Henry did not want to start. He looked to see how much money he had. Then he stood thinking.

At last he said, "I don't want to leave you girls alone."

"Oh," said Jessie, "we'll be all right, Henry. We'll have a surprise for you when you come back. You just wait and see!"

"Good-bye, Henry," said Benny.

So Henry walked off through the woods.

When he had gone, Jessie said, "Now, children, what do you think we are going to do? What do you think I saw over in the woods? I saw some blueberries!"

"Oh, oh!" cried Benny. "I know what blueberries are. Can we have blueberries and milk, Jessie?"

"Yes," Jessie was beginning. But she suddenly stopped, for she heard a noise. Crack, crack, crack! Something was in the woods.

26

Chapter 4

Henry Has Two Surprises

JESSIE WHISPERED, "Keep still!"

The three children did not say a word. They sat quietly in the boxcar, looking at the bushes.

"I wonder if it's a bear," thought Benny.

Soon something came out. But it wasn't a bear. It was a dog, which hopped along on three legs, crying softly and holding up a front paw.

"It's all right," said Jessie. "It's only a dog, but I think he is hurt."

The dog looked up and saw the children, and then he wagged his tail.

"Poor dog," said Jessie. "Are you lost? Come over here and let me look at your paw."

The dog hopped over to the boxcar, and the children got out.

Jessie looked at the paw and said, "Oh dear! You poor dog! There is a big thorn in your foot."

The dog stopped crying and looked at Jessie.

"Good dog," said Jessie. "I can help you, but maybe it will hurt."

The dog looked up at Jessie and wagged his tail again.

"Violet," ordered Jessie, "please wet my handkerchief in the brook."

Jessie sat down on the stump and took the dog in her lap. She patted him and gave him a little piece of bread. Then she began to pull out the thorn. It was a long thorn, but the dog did not make any noise. Jessie pulled and pulled, and at last the thorn came out.

Violet had a wet handkerchief ready. Jessie put it around the dog's paw, and he looked up at her and wagged his tail a little.

"He wants to say 'thank you,' Jessie!" cried Violet. "He is a good dog not to cry."

"Yes, he is," agreed Jessie. "Now I had better hold him for a while so that he will lie down and rest his leg."

28

"We can surprise Henry," remarked Benny. "Now we have a dog."

"So we can," said Jessie. "But that was not my surprise. I was going to get a lot of blueberries for supper."

"Can't we look for blueberries, while you hold the dog?" asked Violet.

"Yes, you can," said Jessie. "Look over there by the big trees."

Benny and Violet ran over to look.

"Oh, Jessie!" cried Benny. "Did you ever see so many blueberries? I guess five blueberries! No, I guess ten blueberries!"

Jessie laughed. "I guess there are more than five or ten, Benny," she said. "Get a clean towel and pick them into it."

For a while Jessie watched Benny and Violet picking blueberries.

"Most of Benny's blueberries are going into his mouth," she thought with a laugh. "But maybe that's just as well. He won't get so hungry waiting for Henry to come back with the milk."

She carried the dog over to the children and sat down beside them, the dog on her lap. With her help, the towel was soon full of blueberries.

"I wish we had some dishes," Jessie said. "Then we could have blueberries and milk."

"Never mind," said Violet. "When Henry comes, we can eat some blueberries and then take a drink of milk."

When Henry came, he had some heavy bundles. He had four bottles of milk in a bag, a loaf of brown bread, and also some fine yellow cheese.

He looked at the dog.

"Where did you get that fine dog?" he cried.

"He came to us," said Benny. "He is a surprise for you."

Henry went over to the dog, who wagged his tail. Henry patted him and said, "He ought to be a good watchdog. Why is the handkerchief on his foot?"

"He had a big thorn in his foot," answered Violet, "and Jessie took it out and put on the handkerchief. It hurt him, but he did not cry or growl."

"His name is Watch," remarked Benny.

31

"Oh, is it?" asked Jessie, laughing. "Watch is a good name for a watchdog."

"Did you bring some milk?" asked Benny, looking hungrily at the bottles.

"I should say I did!" replied Henry. "Four bottles!"

"Poor old Benny!" said Jessie. "We'll have dinner now. Or is it supper?"

"It must be supper," said Henry, "for soon we'll have to go to bed."

"Tomorrow we'll eat three times," said Jessie.

Now Jessie liked to have things in order, and so she put the laundry bag on some pine needles for a tablecloth. Then she cut the loaf of brown bread into five big pieces. The cheese was cut into four.

"Dogs don't like cheese," remarked Benny. The poor little boy was glad too, for he was very hungry.

Violet put the four bottles of milk on the table, and Jessie put some blueberries and cheese at each place.

"Blueberries!" cried Henry. "Jessie, you had *two* surprises for me!"

"I'm sorry we haven't any cups," Jessie said. "We'll have to drink out of the bottles. Now all come and sit down."

So supper began. "Look, Benny," said Henry. "You take some blueberries, then eat some brown bread, then some cheese, then take a drink of milk."

"It's good!" said Benny. He began to put more blueberries into his mouth.

The dog had supper too. Jessie gave him bread as he lay on the ground beside her, and he drank milk out of her hand.

When supper was over, there was some milk left in each bottle.

"We'll have the rest of the milk for breakfast," said Jessie. "Tonight we are going to sleep on beds. Let's get some pine needles now."

Soon the children had a big pile. Henry jumped into the boxcar, and Jessie gave him the pine needles. He made four beds in one end of the car.

"This side is the bedroom," said Jessie.

"What will the other side be?" asked Benny.

"The other side?" asked Jessie. "Let me think. I guess that will be the sitting room, and maybe some of the time it will be the kitchen."

Then she said, "Come, now. Come and get washed." She took the cake of soap and went down to the brook.

"That will be fun, Benny," said Violet. "We'll splash our 'paws' in the brook just as Little Brown Bear does." She knew that Benny did not like to be washed.

The children were all very hot, and so they were glad to splash in the cold water. Benny put cold water and soap on his face with the others and dried his hands on a towel.

"We'll have to have a line to dry the towels on," said Jessie.

So she took the string out of the laundry bag and tied one end of it to a tree. The other end of the string she tied to the boxcar. This made a good clothesline. When she had washed one towel and Violet had washed the other one, they hung both towels on the clothesline.

"It looks like home," said Henry. "See the washing!" He laughed.

34

Jessie was thinking.

"We ought to get some water to drink before we go to bed," she said. "But what shall we put it in?"

"Let's put all the milk into two bottles," said Henry. "Then we can fill the other two with water."

"Good," said Jessie. "You go alone to the fountain, Henry. You can hide if anyone comes along."

Henry went out very quietly, and soon came back with two bottles full of cold water. Benny drank a little, but he was almost asleep.

The other children helped him into the boxcar. Then they all climbed in, Jessie carrying the dog. He lay down at once beside her.

"It is so hot that we'll leave the door open," said Henry.

Soon they were fast asleep, dog and all. The moon came up, but they did not see it. This was the first time in four days that they could go to sleep at night, as children should.

36

Chapter 5

The Explorers Find Treasure

THE NEXT MORNING Jessie woke up first, and she got up at once, for she was the housekeeper. The dog sat in the door of the car and looked at her as she jumped down to get the milk for breakfast. Then he jumped down after her.

Jessie walked down by the little brook and stopped to look at the waterfall. It was beautiful.

"I must look in the refrigerator," she said with a laugh.

It was a funny refrigerator. There was a rock behind the waterfall, and the night before, Jessie had put the two bottles of milk in a hole in this rock. Now she took out the bottles and found that the milk was very cold.

"Is it good?" called Benny, who sat in the car door.

"It is delicious!" cried Jessie. "It is cold too."

She got up into the car with the milk and sat down beside Benny. Then the four children drank the milk for breakfast.

Henry said, "Today I'll go to town and try to get some work to do. I can cut grass or work in a garden or something. Then we'll have something besides milk for breakfast."

He washed his hands and face and started out.

"I'm so glad you have a dog, Jessie," he said. "Good-bye! I'll be back at noon."

The children looked after Henry, and then they looked at Jessie.

"What are we going to do now, Jessie?" Benny asked his sister.

"Well, Benny," answered Jessie, "we'll go exploring and look for treasures. We'll begin here at the car and look and look until we find a dump."

"What's a dump?" asked Benny.

"Oh, Benny!" said Violet. "You know what a dump is. Old tin cans and old dishes and bottles."

"Are old tin cans and dishes treasures?" Benny wanted to know.

"They will be treasures for us," answered Jessie, laughing.

"And wheels?" asked Benny again. "Will there be any wheels on the dump?"

"Yes, maybe," replied Violet. "But cups, Benny, and plates and maybe spoons. You like to drink milk out of a cup."

"Oh yes," agreed Benny politely. But anyone could see that his mind was still on wheels.

The explorers started walking down the old rusty tracks, with Watch hopping along on three legs. The other paw, still tied up with Jessie's handkerchief, was held off the ground. But the dog looked very happy. He liked these kind children.

They all walked along through the woods, looking this way and that. After a while the old track came out into the sun, and the explorers found that they were on top of a hill. They could look down and see the town below them.

"Henry is down there," said Jessie.

Benny was walking along behind his two sisters.

Suddenly he cried happily, "Look, Jessie! There's a treasure—a wheel!"

The girls looked where he was pointing, and they saw

a big dump with many old bottles and tin cans on it. There were also both wheels and cups. Indeed, there were dishes of all kinds.

"Oh, Benny!" cried Jessie. "You saw the treasures first. What should we do without you!"

Violet ran over to the dump. "Here's a white pitcher, Jessie!" she cried.

Jessie looked at it. It was all right, with only one small crack.

"Here's a big white cup too," she said, happily.

"Can you use a teapot, Jessie?" asked Benny.

"Yes, indeed!" she replied. "We can put water in it. I have found two cups and a bowl. Let's look for spoons too!"

Violet held up what she had found—five spoons, covered with rust.

"Good!" said Jessie. "Here's a big kettle. Let's pile all the dishes in it. Then we can carry them back to the boxcar."

Benny had found four wheels just alike and laid them to one side. Now he held up a pink cup. There was a big crack in it, but it had a handle.

41

"This will be my pink cup," said Benny.

"I hope it will hold milk," said Jessie, laughing. "It's a beautiful cup, Benny."

The children laid all their treasures, even the wheels, on a board, and the girls carried the board back to the boxcar between them. They put the dishes down by the brook.

"Now we must wash them," said Jessie.

"All right," agreed Benny. "We'll wash my pink cup."

And never did a little boy hand dishes so carefully to his sisters as Benny did.

The girls washed the dishes with soap, and Jessie used sand to get the rust off the spoons.

"There!" she said, washing the last shining spoon. "How fine they look! But I'm afraid they still aren't clean enough to eat from. When Henry comes, we'll get him to build a fire. Then we can have hot water to rinse them, and they will be *very* clean."

The children sat back and admired the dishes.

Suddenly Violet cried, "Oh, I know where to put them. Come and see what I found in the car last night."

Both girls looked in at the door.

"Look on the door on the other side of the car," said Violet.

All Jessie saw were two pieces of wood nailed to the closed door of the car. But she knew at once what was in Violet's mind. She ran to get the board they had carried from the dump and laid it carefully across the two pieces of wood. It made a fine shelf for the dishes.

"There!" said Jessie.

The children could hardly wait to put the shining dishes on the shelf.

"Let's put them on now," said Violet, "and see how they look, without waiting to rinse them."

When they were on the shelf, Violet picked some white and yellow flowers and put them in a cup full of water in the middle of the shelf.

"There!" said Jessie, stepping back to look at it.

"You said 'there' three times," remarked Benny happily.

"So I did," replied Jessie, laughing. "And I'm going to say it again."

She pointed into the woods and said, "There!"

Henry was coming through the woods, and he carried many funny-looking bundles in his arms. But he would not open his bundles or tell what he had been doing until it was time for dinner.

"Where did you get the dishes?" he cried, when he saw the shelf.

"We went exploring," said Violet, "and found a big dump."

The children began telling him about their treasures. Benny told him about the tin cans and his pink cup and his wheels. Jessie took out the big kettle and asked him about building a fire.

"We want to use the dishes to eat from," she told him, "and it's hard to get them clean in cold water."

So Henry made a small fire in an open place where it could not burn anything. He put big stones all around it.

"We ought to have a fireplace," he remarked.

Jessie cleaned the kettle with sand and filled it with water. Then Henry put it on the fire. Soon the water was boiling, and Jessie rinsed the dishes carefully.

"Now I know they're clean enough to eat from," she said happily.

Chapter 6

A Queer Noise in the Night

AT LAST IT WAS dinnertime, and the children sat down to see what Henry had in his bundles.

"I bought another loaf of brown bread at the store," said Henry, "and some more milk. Then I bought some dried meat, because we can eat it in our hands. And I bought a bone for Watch."

Watch looked hungrily at the bone and lay down at once to eat it.

Jessie got out four cups and bowls and put some milk into each one. Then the children put in little pieces of brown bread and began to eat it with their new spoons.

"What fun!" cried Jessie. "Eating with spoons. Now tell us what you did in town, Henry."

Henry began, "The town below this hill is Silver City. I saw the name on a sign.

47

"I went into the town and walked along the first street I came to. It was a nice street, with big houses and flowers and trees. I saw a man out cutting his grass. He's a good man, too, I can tell you—a doctor."

"Did you work for him?" asked Jessie.

"Yes," said Henry. "He was very hot, and just as I came to the house, his bell rang. He started to the house, and I called after him and asked him if I could cut the grass. He said, 'Yes, yes! I wish you would!' You see, he wasn't used to cutting it himself.

"So I cut the grass, and he said, 'Good for you. Do you want to work every day?' And he said he had never had a boy who cut it as well as I did."

"Oh, Henry!" cried Violet and Jessie.

"I told him I did want to work, and he told me to come back this afternoon.

"He has a pretty house and a garage and a big vegetable garden. Then he has a lot of cherry trees behind the house—a cherry orchard. You should see the beautiful big red cherries!

"Well, when I was cutting the grass near the kitchen, the cook came to the kitchen door and watched me.

"She asked me if I liked cookies. I said I did, and she gave me one."

"What did you do with it?" asked Benny hungrily.

"When she went back into the kitchen, I put it in my pocket," said Henry laughing.

"Did she see you?" cried Jessie.

"Oh no," said Henry. "I played I was eating it. For a long time, I carefully ate away on nothing at all."

Benny began to look at Henry's pocket. It did look very funny.

Henry went on. "When I came home, the doctor gave me a dollar, and the cook gave me this bag."

Henry laughed at Benny and pulled the bag out of his pocket. In it were ten delicious brown cookies.

"Oh, oh!" cried Benny. "Please, Jessie! Let's have cookies for dinner."

"Yes, indeed," said Jessie.

Then Henry opened his last bundle.

49

"I thought we ought to have a tablecloth," he said. "So I got one at the store. But it wasn't hemmed."

Violet begged, "Oh, let me hem it."

She took her scissors out of her workbag and cut the two ends even. But before she began to hem the pretty blue table-cloth, she helped Jessie wash and rinse the dishes and put them away. Benny helped too. When Henry said good-bye and went back to town, all the children were working happily.

Watch was trying to make a hole with one paw to bury his bone in.

"I'll help you bury your bone, Watch," said Benny.

"Oh no, Benny," said Jessie. "Watch wants to bury his bone himself. You come and help me. I'm going to make a broom for the house."

For a little while, Benny ran around finding sticks for the broom, but he soon went to sleep on the ground with the dog for a pillow.

The two girls sat by the brook. Violet was hemming the blue tablecloth, and Jessie was making the broom with a long stick for a handle.

When Henry came back at suppertime, the broom with its long handle stood in the kitchen, and the new tablecloth was hemmed. Henry admired the broom and the tablecloth. Then he gave Jessie a small bundle.

"Oh, butter!" cried Jessie, her eyes shining.

It was butter, yellow and sweet. The four children had not had any butter for many days. At last they sat down to their fine supper.

"Now this spoon is a magic spoon," said Henry. "Turn it around and use the handle, and it is a knife!"

He showed Benny how to put the butter on the brown bread with his magic knife. With dried meat, bread and butter, milk, and cookies, the children could not ask for a better supper.

"What did you do this afternoon, Henry?" asked Jessie.

"Well, I washed the doctor's car," said Henry. "Then I washed the walks and the windows. Tomorrow I'm going to work in the garden."

Then he looked at the brook. "Oh, how I would love to have a swim in that nice cold water!"

Henry was hot and sticky as he looked at the waterfall.

"Maybe we could make a swimming pool," he said. "We could build a dam out of logs."

"Oh yes, we could," said Jessie. "Violet and I know where to find some logs and some big flat stones."

"You do?" said Henry.

"Yes," said Jessie. "They are not far away. And just a little way below here is a pool now, with sand all around it. But it is not big enough to swim in."

"Is that so!" cried Henry. "Someday I'll stay at home, and I'll try to dam up the brook and make a swimming pool."

"You can have my wheels," said Benny.

"Good!" replied Henry. "I'll make you a little cart with the wheels, Benny, and you can carry stones in it."

"Yes," said Benny. "I will."

"Come now, we must go to bed," said Jessie.

The children were all glad to go to bed. They stood on the stump and climbed into their new house, and they all went to sleep but Henry. He was thinking about the

52

new swimming pool. All at once he saw that Watch was not asleep.

Henry patted the dog and said, "Lie down, Watch."

But Watch did not lie down. He began to growl softly.

"Sh!" said Henry to the dog. He sat up. Jessie sat up.

"What is it, Henry?" she whispered.

"I don't know," replied Henry. He was frightened. "I think Watch hears something in the woods."

"Let's close the door," said Jessie. "I'm afraid."

The two children closed the heavy door softly. Then they sat still and listened, but they did not hear anything.

"Lie down, Watch," said Jessie again. "Go to sleep."

But Watch did not go to sleep. He growled again.

"Maybe someone is in the woods. Maybe someone wants to hide in this car," whispered Jessie.

"Maybe," said Henry. "There is something out there that the dog doesn't like."

Then they heard a stick crack, and Watch barked.

"Oh, sh!" Jessie put her hand over his mouth.

"If there is someone out in the woods, he knows that

there is a dog in this boxcar," said Henry.

He took the new broom in his hand and waited.

But nothing came. Nothing at all. The two children waited and waited. Violet and Benny slept through it all.

"I'm going to open the door now," said Henry.

They opened the door softly and then listened. The dog sniffed a little. Then he turned around three times and lay down. He put his head on his paws.

"It must be all right now," said Henry. "Watch knows. Maybe it was just a rabbit."

So at last they all went to sleep and slept until morning.

Chapter 7

A Big Meal from Little Onions

THE NEXT MORNING Jessie and Henry talked about the queer noise. They did not tell Violet and Benny.

"What do you think it was?" asked Jessie. "Do you think it was a rabbit?"

"I don't know," said Henry. "But I think someone was in the woods. I am glad we weren't hurt. Someone must have stepped on a stick and made it crack."

"What shall we do?" asked Jessie.

"Nothing," said Henry. "Watch is a good watchdog. He loves us now, and if anyone tried to hurt us, Watch would take care of us. He would do more than growl. But after this, we must not let Benny go into the woods alone."

"I'll keep Benny and Violet with me all the time," said Jessie.

"Good!" said Henry. "And keep Watch with you all the time too."

"Good morning, Benny. Time to get up. Today you must build something for me out of stones."

"What is it?" asked Benny eagerly.

"I'm not going to tell you," said Henry, laughing.

"You build it just as Jessie tells you, and you will see."

Henry was so eager to begin work that he ran all the way to town. The doctor came to the door and smilingly looked him over from head to foot.

"My mother will tell you what to do today," the doctor said. "She wants you to work in her garden."

Mrs. Moore, the doctor's mother, had a sweet face and looked very kind.

"Good morning, Henry," she said. "Do you know how to thin out vegetables?"

"Oh yes," said Henry. "I like to work in a vegetable garden."

"I haven't had much time to take care of my garden," Mrs. Moore said. "There! See that?"

58

She pulled out a carrot. It had to come out, for it was much too near the other carrots.

"Yes, I see," said Henry.

He began to thin out the carrots. Mrs. Moore watched him as he pulled out some of the little carrots and put them in a pile. He left the other carrots to grow. Then he began on the turnips.

"You are a good worker," said Mrs. Moore. "I can see that." She smiled at Henry. "You may thin out all these vegetables."

Then she went into the house and left Henry alone. He worked all the morning. He thinned out the carrots, turnips, and little onions.

The mill bells rang at noon, but Henry did not hear them. He still worked on in the hot sun. Then he saw Mrs. Moore looking at him.

"You have worked long enough now," she said. "You may come again this afternoon."

"What shall I do with the vegetables I pulled up?" Henry asked.

59

"Oh, I don't want them," said Mrs. Moore. "Just leave them in a pile."

"Do you mind if I take them?" asked Henry.

"No, indeed. Do you have chickens?" Then, without waiting for an answer, she went right on, "You have done good work. Here is a dollar."

Henry said "thank you" and was glad he did not have to answer about the chickens.

When Mrs. Moore went into the house, he took some of the little carrots and turnips and onions. If he had looked up, he would have seen Mrs. Moore in the window watching him. But he did not look up. He was too eager to get to the store and order some meat.

When he arrived at the boxcar, Benny told him, "The building is done. I helped with it."

The "building" was a fireplace, made of flat stones.

"Benny did a lot of the work," said Jessie. "He carried stones and found wood for the fire."

The fireplace was a very good one. The children and Watch had made a hole at the foot of a big rock between

60

two trees. Flat stones were laid on the floor of this hole and around the sides. More big stones were put up to keep out the wind.

Jessie had found a heavy wire in the dump and had put the big kettle on it and tied the ends of the wire to the two trees. The kettle hung over the fireplace, and the fire was laid. Beside the fireplace was a big woodpile.

"Fine! Fine!" cried Henry. "You have done well. Now see what I have."

The girls were delighted with the meat and the little vegetables. With Henry's knife they cut the meat into little pieces. Then they filled the kettle with water from the fountain and put the meat into it, with a tin plate for a cover. Henry started the fire, and it burned well at once.

Jessie cut the tops off the vegetables and washed them in the brook.

"I'll put them in after the meat has cooked awhile," she said.

Soon the water began to boil, and the stew began to smell good. Watch sat down and looked at it. He sniffed

hungrily at it and barked and barked.

The children sat around the fireplace, eating bread and milk. Now and then Jessie stirred the stew with a big spoon.

"It will make a good meal," said Henry. "Keep it boiling and do not leave it. When I come home tonight, I'll bring you some salt. And whatever you do, don't get on fire!"

Violet pointed to the pitcher and teapot that she had filled with water.

"That's to put on Benny or Watch if he should get on fire," she said.

Henry laughed and went happily on his way. He wished he could stay and smell the stew boiling, but he thought he ought to work. So he went back to Dr. Moore's house.

He was very happy when Dr. Moore said, "Do you want to clean up this garage?"

The garage was not in very good order. Dr. Moore laughed when he saw Henry look around for a broom.

"I must go out now," said Dr. Moore. "You just clean this place up."

Henry began at once. First he opened all the boxes. On the biggest box he painted the word *TOOLS* with a long-handled brush and a can of paint he had found. On another box he painted *NAILS*. Then he picked over the things and put the tools in the toolbox and the nails in the nail box. This was fun for Henry, because he liked to get things in order.

Henry found a lot of nails that were bent and covered with rust. He put them in his pocket.

"I'll ask the doctor for these bent nails," he said to himself. "They are no good to him, but they are fine for me. I can use every old nail I get."

Then he washed the floor and washed his paintbrush.

When Dr. Moore came home, he found Henry putting brushes, paint cans, and other things on the shelf.

"My, my, my!" he cried. He looked at the garage and laughed and laughed. He laughed until his mother came out to see what he was laughing at.

"Look, Mother!" he said. "Look at those tools. Look at the shelf. Look at my hammers. One, two, three, four hammers.

Your hammer, my hammer, and two other hammers. They were all lost. Can you use a hammer, Henry?"

"Yes, indeed I can!" cried Henry.

"Take one," said Dr. Moore. "You found them all."

"Oh, thank you!" said Henry. He showed the doctor the bent nails, and was told that he could have those too. He could hardly wait now to start home, because he was so eager to show Benny and his sisters his new hammer and nails.

"Tomorrow will be Sunday," said Dr. Moore. "Will you come again the next day?"

"Oh yes," replied Henry, who had lost all track of the days.

"The cherries must be picked," said the doctor. He looked at Henry in a queer way. "We could use any number of cherry pickers if they were all as careful as you."

"Could you?" asked Henry eagerly. "Well, I'll come."

So the three said good-bye, and Henry started for home. He had another dollar, a pocket full of old nails, a hammer, and the pile of vegetables that he had left at noon. On the way home he bought some salt.

When he arrived at the boxcar, he began to smell a delicious smell.

"Onions!" he shouted, running up to the kettle. "I do like the smell of onions."

"I like the turnips best," said Violet.

Jessie took off the cover carefully and stirred in the salt, and Henry sniffed the brown stew. It was boiling and boiling.

"A ladle, of all things!" cried Henry. "Where did you get it?"

"I found a tin cup in the dump," said Jessie. "We used a long stick for a handle and tied it to the cup with a piece of wire. It makes a fine ladle."

She ladled out the stew into plates and bowls and put a spoon in each one.

"Oh, oh!" said Benny. "I am so hungry. I must eat my supper!"

The meat was well cooked, and the vegetables were delicious. Violet passed her plate for more turnips.

66

"I'd like some more onions," said Henry.

All the children ate until they could eat no more.

"That was the best meal I ever ate," said Jessie.

"Me too," said Violet.

"I have time tonight to make Benny's cart," remarked Henry. "We'll want a cart."

"Will you make it with my wheels?" asked Benny.

"Yes, with your wheels," answered Henry. "But you must cart stones in it when I get it done."

"Yes," said Benny. "I will cart stones or rocks or anything."

"Tomorrow will be Sunday, and I can stay at home," Henry went on. "Do you think it's all right, Jessie, to build the dam for a swimming pool on Sunday?"

"Yes, I do," said Jessie. "We are making the swimming pool so that we can keep clean."

Henry began happily to hammer out the bent nails with his new hammer. Soon he had some good nails.

"You and I will go and find some boards, Benny," he said. "Come on."

Soon the boys came back with some boards from the dump. Henry sat down and began to make the cart. He could not see very well, because it was getting dark and there was no moon. But at last the cart was done, and he gave it to Benny.

"Thank you," said Benny, politely.

After his sisters had admired the cart, Benny pulled it around just for fun. Then Henry put it in the boxcar for the night.

Henry said to Jessie, "I hope we do not hear that queer noise tonight."

"I hope not too," said Jessie. Then she laughed. "Look at Benny," she said. "He has gone to sleep with his hand on his cart."

Henry laughed too, but he laughed at himself, because he was going to sleep with his new hammer under his pillow.

69

Chapter 8

A Swimming Pool at Last

THE BOXCAR CHILDREN were so tired that they slept until ten o'clock Sunday morning.

When they woke up at last, they hurried through breakfast and went to work on the swimming pool.

"We'll make a dam across the brook," said Henry.

"Here is my cart," said Benny. "I'll cart stones and logs in it."

"Good for you," laughed Henry.

First the four children went down the brook to look at the pool Jessie had seen. The water was quiet here, and there was clean sand all around the little pool.

"It's big enough for a swimming pool," Henry remarked, "but I don't think it's deep enough."

He put a long stick in it to see how deep it was. When he looked at the wet stick, he found that the water was about a foot deep.

"The swimming pool should be three times as deep," he said. "Then it will be deep enough to swim in and won't be too deep for Benny. We'll build the dam here with logs and stones."

While the other children started the dam, Jessie washed all their stockings.

"We won't want our stockings on while we are working in the brook," she remarked, as she rinsed them and hung them on the clothesline to dry. "So this is a good time to wash them."

It was hard work building the dam, but the children liked hard work. Henry and Jessie pulled the logs to the brook, and Violet and Benny carried the stones, with the help of the cart. Now and then Henry was called on to help with a heavy stone. But the two younger children carried most of them.

"Splash the stones right into the water," Henry told them. "But be careful to keep them in a line between these two trees."

The children watched with delighted eyes as the wall of stones under the water began to grow higher and higher.

"The rock wall will help to hold the logs in place," said Henry.

At last it was time to lay the logs across the brook.

"Let's lay the first ones between these two trees," said Jessie. "Then the trees will hold both ends of the logs."

"Good work!" cried Henry, much pleased. "That's just what we'll do."

But when the first big log was splashed into place on top of the stone wall, the water began to run over the top of the log and around both ends.

"Oh dear!" cried Jessie. "The water runs around the ends every time! What shall we do?"

"We'll have to put lots of logs on, with brush between them," said Henry. "We'll put on so many that the water *can't* get through."

They laid three logs across, with three more on top of them, and three more on top of those. Violet filled her arms with brush and held it in place until each log was

laid. Benny filled the holes at the ends of the logs with flat stones. Such wet children never were seen before, but the hot sun would dry them off, and no one cared.

When the three top logs were laid in place at last, the four tired children sat down to watch the pool fill. But Henry could not sit still as the water came higher and higher up the dam.

"See how deep the pool is getting!" he cried. "See how still it is!"

At last the pool was full, and the water came over the top of the dam and made another waterfall.

"Just like a mill dam!" said Henry. "Now the pool is deep enough for all of us to swim in."

"You boys can have the first swim," said Jessie. "We girls must go and get dinner. We'll ring the bell when we are ready."

The boys splashed around in the pool, while the girls made a fire and hung the kettle of brown stew over it, stirring it now and then. Violet cut the bread and then got the butter, hard and cold, out of the refrigerator.

When everything was ready, Jessie rang the dinner bell. This bell was only a tin can from the dump. Jessie had hung it on a tree with a string, and she rang it with a spoon. Then she got the ladle and began ladling out the stew.

"That's the dinner bell," said Benny. "I know it is. Come, Watch. Don't you want some dinner?"

Watch had had a swim too. He came out of the water and shook himself. The two boys put on their dry clothes and went to Sunday dinner.

"Let me ring the bell again," said Benny.

"I like stew even better today," said Henry, eating hungrily.

"That's because we worked so hard," remarked Jessie. "Let's go for a walk in the woods this afternoon."

"Oh, let's!" cried Violet. "Let's go exploring again."

The children washed the dishes and then started on their walk.

As they went along, Watch began to bark. At first the explorers were frightened.

"Oh, what is it?" cried Violet.

"Maybe it's a rabbit," said Henry.

Then they saw a hen running away through the woods. Watch ran after her, but Henry called him back.

"Don't run after the poor hen," he said.

"The hen had a nest," remarked Benny.

"What?" asked Jessie.

"She had some eggs in it," said Benny. "Come here and see."

Jessie looked on the ground where Benny was pointing and saw a nest with five eggs in it.

"A runaway hen!" said Jessie. "She wanted to hide her nest so she would have some chickens. We'll have the eggs for supper. I know how to cook eggs."

The eggs made a delicious supper. Jessie put them in a bowl, with a little salt, and Violet took a spoon and stirred them as hard as she could.

"Put in some milk, Violet," said Jessie, "and stir them some more."

Henry started up the fire. The big kettle was hung over the fire, and Jessie put in some butter. She watched

77

the butter until it was nice and brown, and then she put in the eggs.

"Sit down," she said. "Be all ready to eat when the eggs are done."

Violet put the blue tablecloth on the ground. She got the bread and butter and the plates and spoons, and the children all sat ready for supper.

"Here I come!" cried Jessie. "Hold out your plates."

"Oh, Jessie!" cried Benny. "This is the best meal I ever ate. I found the eggs, and you cooked them."

"Yes, you did, Benny," said Henry. "Thank you for a fine meal."

"Tomorrow we'll have to eat bread and milk," said Jessie.

But when tomorrow came, the children had more than bread and milk, as you will soon see.

80

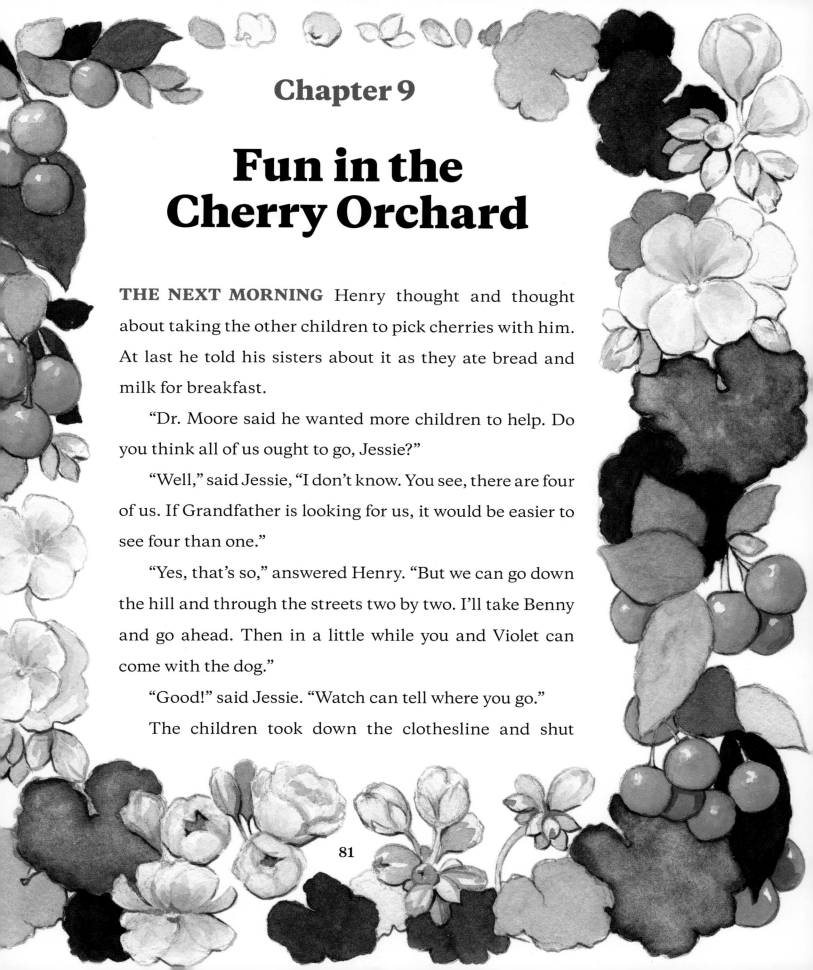

Chapter 9

Fun in the Cherry Orchard

THE NEXT MORNING Henry thought and thought about taking the other children to pick cherries with him. At last he told his sisters about it as they ate bread and milk for breakfast.

"Dr. Moore said he wanted more children to help. Do you think all of us ought to go, Jessie?"

"Well," said Jessie, "I don't know. You see, there are four of us. If Grandfather is looking for us, it would be easier to see four than one."

"Yes, that's so," answered Henry. "But we can go down the hill and through the streets two by two. I'll take Benny and go ahead. Then in a little while you and Violet can come with the dog."

"Good!" said Jessie. "Watch can tell where you go."

The children took down the clothesline and shut

81

the door of the car. Everything was in order. Then they started out.

When they arrived at the orchard, they soon saw that they were not the only workers. The doctor was there, and the cook, and two men carrying ladders and baskets.

"Good morning, Henry," said Mrs. Moore. "Can you work today?"

"Oh yes," said Henry. "These are my sisters, Jessie and Violet. They can pick cherries too. Benny is too young to climb trees, but we had to bring him."

"Maybe he can carry baskets," said Dr. Moore, smiling at Benny. "You see, this is a big cherry year, and we have to work fast, once we begin. Maybe he can help fill the little baskets from the big ones."

"Eat all you want," said Mrs. Moore. "The cherries are beautiful this year."

The children didn't eat all they wanted, but every now and then a big red cherry went into someone's mouth.

Henry and the girls went up the ladders and began to pick cherries. Watch barked for a while. He did not like

to have Jessie climbing the ladder. Then he sat down and looked at her up in the tree.

Benny hurried here and there, carrying baskets to the pickers and eating all the cherries he wanted. Everyone in the orchard liked Benny. The doctor laughed delightedly at him, and sweet Mrs. Moore fell in love with him at once. By and by he sat down beside her and carefully filled small baskets with cherries from the big baskets.

The men laughed at the funny things Benny said, and Watch barked happily. By and by the doctor left the orchard to make some calls.

At last Mrs. Moore said, "I never had such happy cherry pickers before. You are having such a good time out here that I don't want to go in the house." She smiled.

Mary, the cook, seemed to think the same thing, for she came again and again into the orchard.

After a while the cook went in to get dinner, but the children still picked cherries. At noon Dr. Moore came home.

"You must stay to dinner," he said to the children. "We can eat here in the orchard under the trees. Will your mother be watching for you?" When he asked this, he looked at Henry in a queer way.

Henry did not know what to say. But at last Jessie said, "No. Our mother and father are dead."

"Then you must stay," said Mrs. Moore. "Here comes Mary."

The cook put a table under the trees, and they all sat around it and ate a delicious dinner. Then Mary went into the house and came out again with big bowls of cherry dumplings.

"I can smell something good!" cried Benny. "Is it cherries?"

"Yes, my little dear," said Mary. "Cherry dumplings. The cherries are cooked in the dumplings."

Benny ate his cherry dumpling and then went to sleep with the dog for a pillow. But Henry and Jessie and Violet began to work again. Mrs. Moore looked out of the window at them.

"Just see how those children work," she said to Dr. Moore. "And they are so polite too. I wonder who they are."

Dr. Moore said nothing. After a while he went out to the orchard. "You have worked long enough," he said.

He gave them four dollars and all the cherries they could carry.

"That is too much," said Henry.

"No," said Dr. Moore, "it is just right. You see, you are better than most workers, because you are so happy. Come again."

"I'll come every day," said Benny.

They all laughed.

Dr. Moore saw that the children did not all leave the orchard at the same time, but started down the street two by two.

"I wish I knew who they are," he said to himself.

When the cherry pickers got back to their little home, they looked everything over carefully. But things were just as they had left them. The door was still closed, and the milk and butter were in the refrigerator. The children made a happy supper of bread and butter and cherries and then went to bed in the boxcar.

That same night, Dr. Moore sat reading the paper. All at once he saw the word *LOST* and began to read.

"Lost. Four children, two boys and two girls. Somewhere around Greenfield or Silver City. Five thousand dollars to anyone who can find them.

James Henry Alden."

Dr. Moore sat up. "Five thousand dollars!" he said. "James Henry Alden! Oh my! Oh my!"

He sat still for a long time, thinking and laughing to himself.

"The four children are living in a boxcar, but I shall not tell Mr. Alden that they are his grandchildren," he said.

Chapter 10

Henry and the Free-for-All

JAMES HENRY ALDEN was a very rich man. His big mills stood just between Greenfield and Silver City.

Now J. H. Alden liked boys. He liked to see them running and jumping and playing. So each year, with three other rich men, he gave a field day to the town of Silver City. And even the mills were closed on Field Day.

Every year the boys were in training for the races. And not only boys, but men also, thin and fat, and girls trained for Field Day.

There were prizes for all kinds of races—running and swimming and jumping.

But the best one was a footrace, called a free-for-all, because anyone could run in it. Mr. Alden gave a prize of twenty-five dollars and a silver cup to the winner of the free-for-all. Sometimes a boy won the race, sometimes a

girl. Once a fat man had won it.

On Field Day Henry was cutting the grass for Dr. Moore. Suddenly the doctor stopped his car in the street and called to Henry.

"Hop in," he said. "Today is Field Day, and I want you to see the races."

Henry hopped in, and the doctor started the car.

"I'm sorry I can't go," said Dr. Moore, "and I want to know all about it. I want you to tell me who wins each race."

Soon Henry found himself sitting on the bleachers. By and by a small boy climbed up the bleachers and sat beside him. Then a man called, "Free-for-all! Come and get ready!"

"What is that?" asked Henry. "A free-for-all?"

"Don't you know?" asked the small boy. "Didn't you see the one last year?"

"No," said Henry.

The boy laughed. "That was a funny one," he said. "There were two fat men in it, and some girls and boys. That boy over there won it. You should have seen him. He ran so fast you could hardly see his legs at all!"

Henry looked at the winner of last year's race. He was smaller than Henry, but he was older. Suddenly Henry stood up and quietly left the bleachers. He went to the room where the boys were getting ready for the race.

"Do you want to run in the race?" a man asked him.

"Yes, I do," replied Henry.

The man gave him some track clothes to put on.

"Where did you train?" he asked.

"I never was trained," said Henry.

"These boys have been training all year," remarked the man.

"Oh, I don't think I'll win," answered Henry. "But I like to run. It's lots of fun, you know."

"So it is," said the man. "So it is."

Henry could hardly wait for the race to begin. He loved to run. But at last the race was called. It was time to start. Henry was Number 4.

Now Henry began to think. "It's a long race," he said to himself. "I must go easy at first."

The bell rang. Off went the runners down the track. In almost no time Henry was far behind most of the other runners. But he did not seem to mind this.

"It's fun to run, anyway," he said again to himself. And he tried to see how easily he could run.

All at once he had another thought. "I have tried to see how easily I can run," he said to himself. "Now I'll try to see how fast I can run."

Then all the people began to see how fast Henry could run. He ran faster and faster, and soon he passed the two girls ahead of him. Then he passed a fat man and a little boy.

The people began to shout, "Number 4! Number 4!" Here was the kind of race they loved!

"Faster, faster!" cried Henry to himself. "I can run faster than this."

He could. He passed Number 25 and Number 6. Then he passed Number 5 and Number 10. Only one runner was ahead of Henry now. It was Number 16. Then Henry began to think of winning the race. He knew how much the

twenty-five-dollar prize would mean to Jessie and the rest of the children.

"I am going to win this race!" he said to himself. "I must pass Number 16."

He ran still faster. He could see the line at the end of the race.

"Number 4! Number 4!" shouted the people. "He is going to win!"

When Henry was near Number 16, he put his head down and ran as fast as he could. He passed Number 16 and went across the line! He had won!

The people shouted and shouted. Some men held Henry up high and carried him to Mr. Alden for the prize.

Then a man asked, "What is your name, boy?"

Henry did not know what to say. He did not want to tell his name. So he answered, "Henry James." Now this was Henry's name, but it was not all of his name.

At once the big sign said,

HENRY JAMES, NUMBER 4

WINNER OF FREE-FOR-ALL

94

"Here is the prize, Henry James," said Mr. Alden. "You can run well, my boy. I like to see you run."

He gave Henry a silver cup and the twenty-five dollars. Then he shook hands with him.

Just then Dr. Moore came along and climbed up in the bleachers, but Henry did not see him. The doctor laughed to himself as Henry James shook hands with James Henry.

At last Henry got away from the people and started back to Dr. Moore's. He had the twenty-five-dollar prize in his pocket. When Dr. Moore came home and found Henry cutting the grass, he laughed quietly to himself.

"I just got home," said Henry. "I will tell you who won all the races."

Dr. Moore did not tell Henry that he had been up in the bleachers. He let Henry tell him about the races.

"And who won the free-for-all?" he asked.

"I did," said Henry.

"You did?" cried Dr. Moore. "Good for you! What are you going to do with the money?"

"I'll give it to Jessie," answered Henry.

"Good," said the doctor again.

When Henry arrived at the boxcar with the twenty-five dollars, he found dinner ready. Jessie had boiled the rest of the vegetables and put butter on top. The children began to eat, but, hungry as they were, they stopped when Henry told them about the race and showed them the silver cup. They were so excited that they couldn't eat.

"You won the race, Henry?" cried Jessie, delighted. "Oh, I'm so glad!"

"You can run fast, Henry," said Benny. "I'm glad you won the race too." He looked at the silver cup.

"I said my name was Henry James," said Henry.

"That's right," said Jessie. "So it is. You didn't have to change it."

"Are we rich now, Henry?" asked Benny.

"No, not very," said Henry, laughing. "By the way, I bought something for supper."

Jessie looked in the bag. There were some fat brown potatoes in it.

"Oh, I know how to cook these!" cried Jessie, happily.

"They will be good. You just wait."

"I can't wait," said Henry, laughing. Then he went back to work.

After dinner, Benny played around with the dog.

"Benny," Jessie said suddenly, as she hung her dish towels up to dry. "It's high time you learned to read."

"No," said Benny. "No school now."

Jessie laughed. "No," she said, "you can't go to school, but I can help you. I wish I had a book."

"We could make a book," said Violet. "We have all the papers left from bundles."

"So we could," replied Jessie. "But what could we use to make the words?"

"We could use a burned stick out of the fire," said Violet.

So Jessie put the end of a long stick into the fire and burned it black. Then she used the burned end to make words.

"Won't Henry be glad when he finds Benny can read?" cried Violet.

Now Benny did not want to learn to read. But he liked

to watch the girls make the book. Jessie made the words *SEE ME* in the book. She called Benny. But he could not tell *see* from *me*.

"Don't you see, Benny?" said Jessie. "This one has an *S*. It says *see*. This one has *M*. It says *me*."

But Benny did not see.

"It is too hard for me," he said.

"I'll tell you, Jessie," said Violet at last. "Let's make *see* on one paper and *me* on the other. That's the way they do in school. Then have him point to *see*."

The girls did this. They called Benny, and Jessie showed him again very carefully the word that said *see*. Then she put the two words down on the ground.

"Now, Benny, point to *see*," said Jessie.

Benny looked at the two words. He could not tell.

But Watch barked and put his paw on *see*.

Now Watch did not know one word from the other, but Benny thought he did. Was he going to let a dog get ahead of him? Not Benny! He looked at the words and learned them almost at once.

"Good old Watch!" said Jessie.

"It isn't hard at all," said Benny. "Is it, Watch?"

Before supper Benny could read:

"See me.

See me run.

I can run.

Can you run?"

"Good boy," said Jessie. "Now I must get supper."

The children started up the fire and washed the potatoes in the brook. Then Jessie put wet papers around them and put them in the fire under the hot stones.

"Are you going to burn them up, Jessie?" asked Benny.

"Oh no, Benny," said Jessie. "You wait and see."

When Henry came home, he found Jessie rolling the potatoes out of the fire. They were very black.

"Oh, did you burn them up?" asked Henry.

"No, indeed," said Jessie. "Come and see." She gave three black potatoes to each one.

"They are very hot," said Violet. "Look out!"

"Open them," said Jessie, "and take out the potato with

a spoon. Then put butter on top and some salt. I will get Benny's out. Well, how are they?"

"Oh!" cried Benny. "They are delicious!"

"What did I tell you?" said Jessie. "Have some milk!"

"Milk and potatoes make a very good supper," said Henry.

"I can read," remarked Benny.

"What!" said Henry.

"Yes, he can," said Violet. "He learned this afternoon. Go and get your book, Benny."

Benny liked to read now. "It is not hard," he said. "Watch can read too."

"Oh, can he?" laughed Henry. "Let's see him."

"Watch is too tired now," said Benny. "I will read to you."

Benny read out of his new book.

"Good old Benny," said Henry. "Come to bed now. You must be tired with all that work, and I am tired too."

100

Chapter 11

The Doctor
Takes a Hand

THE DAYS WENT BY happily for the boxcar children. They found more treasures in the dump, and Henry worked every day for Dr. Moore.

One noon Henry came home with some new stockings for Benny. Benny was very happy about them and made everyone admire them. And when Jessie looked at the new stockings, she had a happy thought.

She carefully washed Benny's old stockings and hung them up to dry. That afternoon she and Violet sat down, with the workbag between them, to make a bear for Benny.

"You must make a tail too, Jessie," begged Benny, watching her put on the arms and legs and head.

"Bears don't have tails," said Jessie. "Your old bear didn't have a tail."

"But this bear must have a tail," replied Benny, knowing

that Jessie would put on two tails if he asked her to.

"What kind of tail?" asked Jessie at last.

"Long and thin," said Benny happily, "so I can pull it."

"Benny!" cried Jessie, laughing.

But she made a tail, long and thin, just as Benny had ordered.

"What's his name, Jessie?" asked Benny, when at last the bear was handed over to him.

"I haven't thought about a name," replied Jessie. "Why don't you think up a nice name for him?"

"Well, you made him out of my old stockings. Let's name him Stockings."

"All right, Stockings it is," agreed Jessie, trying not to laugh.

And from that day on, the bear's name was Stockings as long as he lived. And he lived to be a very old bear, indeed.

One afternoon Jessie saw how long Benny's hair was getting, and she cut it with Violet's scissors. Benny stood quietly while she did it.

But while his sisters were getting supper, he said to

himself, "Jessie cut my hair. I'll get Violet's scissors and cut Watch's hair. He will look better."

He found Violet's scissors and made Watch lie down on his side. Then he began to cut the hair off.

Benny said, "Good dog, Watch. You are Jessie's dog, and so I will cut a *J* in your hair. Hold still now."

Watch lay still, and Benny began to cut a *J*. It was not a very good *J*, but it looked a little like one.

Soon Benny had cut off all the hair on one side, with a *J* in the middle. He stood admiring his work, and just then Jessie came to see what he was doing.

"Benny!" she cried. "What are you doing?" Then she began to laugh.

"Oh, Violet, come and see!" she called. "Watch looks so funny."

Jessie laughed and laughed until she almost cried. Violet laughed until she did cry.

Then she could not stop crying. She cried and cried. At last Jessie made up her mind that Violet was really sick.

"You must go to bed, Violet," she said. She helped her

carefully into the boxcar and put pine needles all around her and under her. Then she wet a handkerchief in the cold water of the brook and laid it on her little sister's hot head.

"I wish Henry would come home!" said Jessie. "What shall we do?"

When Henry came at last, he looked at Violet and said that maybe she had a cold. "Maybe she sat too long by the brook," he said.

"If Violet is very sick, she ought to go to the hospital," said Jessie.

"Yes, I know that," said Henry. "And we don't want her to go to a hospital if we can help it. We should have to tell her name."

"Yes," said Jessie. "Then Grandfather could find us."

The two older children sat up with Violet. They put cold water on her head. But after dark Violet shook all over, and Jessie was frightened. She covered Violet all over with pine needles, but still she shook. They could not get her warm.

"I'm going to get Dr. Moore," said Henry. "I'm afraid Violet is very sick."

Then Henry started to run. He ran even faster than he had run in the race. Down the hill into the town he ran, until he came to Dr. Moore's house.

"Please come!" he cried. "Violet is very sick!"

The doctor said, "Come and get into my car."

He did not ask Henry which way to go, but the car went up the right road. When they came to the woods, he said to Henry, "Stay here in the car."

He ran alone up the hill to the boxcar. It seemed like magic that he knew where to go.

When Dr. Moore came back, he was carrying Violet in his arms. Jessie and Benny and Watch came too. They all got into the car.

"Are you going to take her to a hospital?" asked Henry.

"No," said Dr. Moore. "I'm taking her to my house."

When they stopped at last, Dr. Moore carried Violet into the house and said to his mother, "Violet is very sick. We must put her to bed."

Mrs. Moore hurried around, opening beds and bringing pillows, and Mary came from the kitchen with hot-water

bottles. After a while Violet began to get warm.

Then Mrs. Moore came to get the other children. "You must stay here all night," she said.

She gave Henry and Benny a big bed, and Jessie slept in a little one. But Violet was so sick that the doctor did not go to bed all night. He would not leave her. He sat by her side until ten o'clock in the morning.

Before ten o'clock a man came to see the doctor. Mary told him he could wait. So he sat down in the living room. Soon Benny came in.

"Where *is* the doctor?" asked the man, crossly.

"He is up in Violet's room," answered Benny.

"This means five thousand dollars to him if he will come down," said the man.

"Oh, he can't come now," said Benny.

"What do you mean, boy?" asked the man. "What is he doing?"

"He's taking care of my sister Violet," said Benny. "She is sick."

"And you mean he wouldn't leave her even if I gave him

five thousand dollars?" asked the man.

"Yes," answered Benny. "That's what I mean."

Then the man said, "You see, I have lost a little boy, and I think the doctor knows where he is. My little boy is just about as old as you are."

"Well, if you don't find him, maybe you can have me," remarked Benny. "I like you."

"You do?" cried the man. "Come and get up in my lap."

Benny climbed into the man's lap. "Have you got a dog?" he asked.

"No," said the man. "He is dead now. But you can see him in my watch. Here it is."

Benny looked at the dog. "He looks like a very good dog," he said. "I have a dog too. His name is Watch."

Just then Watch came in with Dr. Moore.

"Good morning," said Dr. Moore. "Benny, you can go and play with Watch."

Benny ran out, and the man said, "Dr. Moore, where are my grandchildren?"

"That little boy is one of them," said Dr. Moore quietly.

"That beautiful little boy!" said the man.

"Yes," said Dr. Moore. "They are all good children. But they are afraid of you. They are afraid you will find them."

"How do you know that?" asked the man.

"They have changed their name," said the doctor. He looked at the man in a queer way. "The big boy changed his name on Field Day. You saw him then."

"I saw him? What did he change his name to?" asked the man.

"Henry James," said the doctor.

"The running boy!" cried the man. "The boy who won the free-for-all! I liked that boy. So I am his grandfather."

112

Chapter 12

James Henry and Henry James

DR. MOORE WENT to get his mother. "Mother," he said, "this is Mr. James Henry Alden. He wants to take his grandchildren to live with him."

"I'm afraid they won't want to go with you," said Mrs. Moore, "until they learn to like you. And they won't want to go while Violet is so sick."

"Can't I see them?" begged Mr. Alden. "I won't tell them who I am."

"That would help," agreed the doctor. "If they grow to like you before they know who you are, things will be easier."

"Yes," said Mrs. Moore. "Stay here with us for a while. The children will learn to like you, and then we can tell them that you are their grandfather."

"Thank you," said Mr. Alden. "I will go home and get

113

some clothes and come back. And I will give you the five thousand dollars."

But Dr. Moore would not take the money.

"I just want these children to be happy," he said.

When Mary learned that she was to cook for Mr. Alden, she was frightened. "How can I cook for him?" she cried. "He has everything. He is a very rich man."

"You can cook for anyone," said Dr. Moore, kindly. "Just get one of your good chicken dinners and make some cherry dumplings."

At dinner Mr. Alden saw all his grandchildren but Violet. He smiled with delight when he saw Jessie come into the room in her quiet way.

"Children," said Mrs. Moore, "this is Mr. Henry."

Benny laughed. "Henry and Mr. Henry," he remarked. "That is funny."

Henry shook hands with Mr. Alden before he sat down at the table.

"Where have I seen that man before?" he thought.

The children liked to hear Mr. Henry talk. He told

them about a big cucumber in his garden. The cucumber was growing inside a bottle, and he couldn't get it out.

"Why not?" asked Benny.

"It is too big," said Mr. Alden.

"How did it get in?" asked Benny.

"It was a little cucumber when it went in," said Mr. Alden. "A cucumber will grow just the same in a bottle. It will grow so big you can't get it out."

"I'd like to see the cucumber," said Benny, stopping in the middle of his cherry dumpling.

"Would you really?" asked Mr. Alden, delighted. "Some day you and I will go over and pick it."

"And we can bring it to Violet," said Benny.

"Yes, we'll bring it to Violet," agreed Mr. Alden.

Henry thought again, "Where have I seen that man before? I wish I could remember."

He could not remember, but he liked Mr. Alden very much. All the children liked him because he was kind to them.

At last, one day, Mr. Alden could see Violet and went

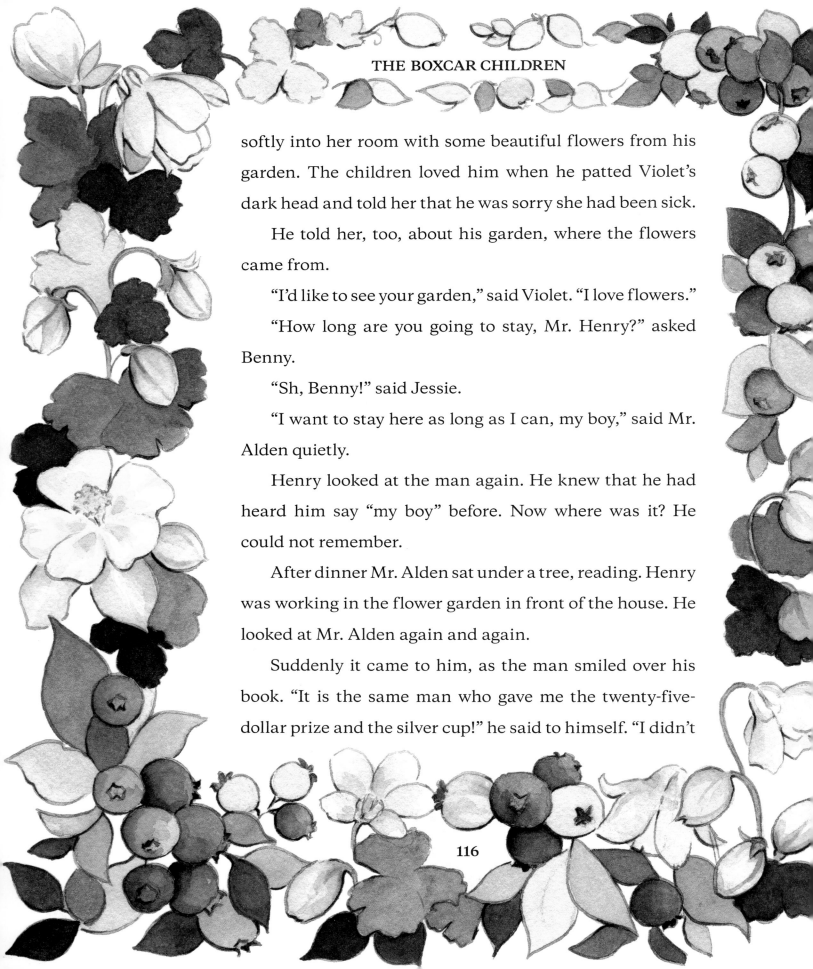

softly into her room with some beautiful flowers from his garden. The children loved him when he patted Violet's dark head and told her that he was sorry she had been sick.

He told her, too, about his garden, where the flowers came from.

"I'd like to see your garden," said Violet. "I love flowers."

"How long are you going to stay, Mr. Henry?" asked Benny.

"Sh, Benny!" said Jessie.

"I want to stay here as long as I can, my boy," said Mr. Alden quietly.

Henry looked at the man again. He knew that he had heard him say "my boy" before. Now where was it? He could not remember.

After dinner Mr. Alden sat under a tree, reading. Henry was working in the flower garden in front of the house. He looked at Mr. Alden again and again.

Suddenly it came to him, as the man smiled over his book. "It is the same man who gave me the twenty-five-dollar prize and the silver cup!" he said to himself. "I didn't

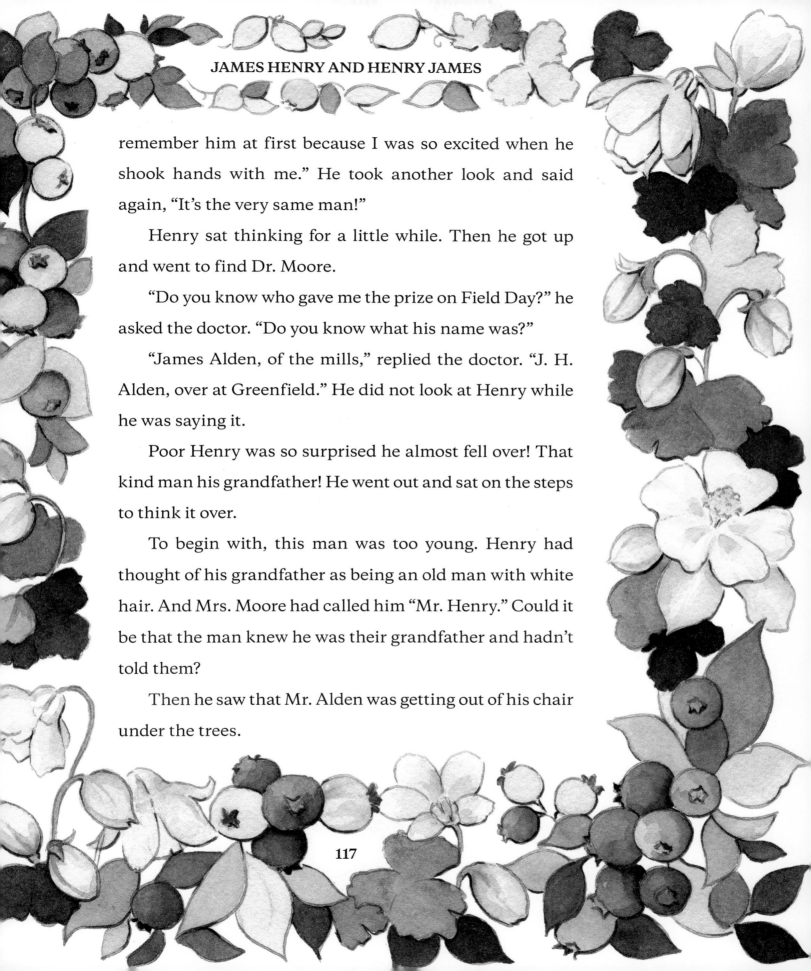

remember him at first because I was so excited when he shook hands with me." He took another look and said again, "It's the very same man!"

Henry sat thinking for a little while. Then he got up and went to find Dr. Moore.

"Do you know who gave me the prize on Field Day?" he asked the doctor. "Do you know what his name was?"

"James Alden, of the mills," replied the doctor. "J. H. Alden, over at Greenfield." He did not look at Henry while he was saying it.

Poor Henry was so surprised he almost fell over! That kind man his grandfather! He went out and sat on the steps to think it over.

To begin with, this man was too young. Henry had thought of his grandfather as being an old man with white hair. And Mrs. Moore had called him "Mr. Henry." Could it be that the man knew he was their grandfather and hadn't told them?

Then he saw that Mr. Alden was getting out of his chair under the trees.

"It's now or never," thought Henry. "I have to know!"

He walked eagerly after the man, who was going toward the garden with his back to Henry. Then the man turned around and saw how excited Henry was.

"Are you James Henry Alden of Greenfield?" Henry asked.

"I am, my boy," replied Mr. Alden, with a smile. "Does that mean *you* know that I know you are Henry James Alden?"

"Yes," said Henry quietly.

Then James Henry Alden shook hands again with Henry James Alden.

Jessie and Benny came across the grass just in time to hear Henry say, "But, Grandfather—"

"Grandfather?" cried Jessie. "What do you mean, Henry?"

"Yes, Jessie," said Henry eagerly. "He's the man we have been running away from all this time."

"I thought you were old," said Benny. "And cross. Jessie said so."

"I didn't know, Benny," said Jessie. Her face was red. To think of running away from this kind man!

But her grandfather did not seem to mind. He patted her on the head and said, "Let's go up and see Violet."

There was no stopping Benny. He hurried into Violet's room, holding Mr. Alden by the hand and shouting, "It's Grandfather, Violet! And he isn't cross after all!"

"What do you mean?" asked Violet. "Isn't he Mr. Henry?"

"My name is James Henry Alden," replied her grandfather.

"And my name is Henry James Alden," cried Henry.

"Well, well!" said Dr. Moore.

Violet held on to her grandfather's hand and listened to the rest talking excitedly.

"*Where* have you been living?" asked Mr. Alden at last.

They all looked at each other, even Dr. Moore and his mother. Then they all laughed as if they never would stop.

"You just ought to see!" said Dr. Moore.

"What!" cried all the children at once. "*You* never saw

it in the daytime."

"Is that so?" laughed the doctor. "I have seen it many times in the daytime."

"Seen what?" asked Mr. Alden.

"Our house," said Jessie. "We have been living in a boxcar in the woods."

Then they all began to tell him about the dump and the dishes and the brook and the swimming pool.

"They have four beds of pine needles in the car," said Dr. Moore.

"How do you know?" asked Jessie.

"Well," said Dr. Moore, "the first day Henry worked for me, I walked after him as far as the hill."

"Why did you do that?" asked Mr. Alden.

"I liked him. I saw he was a fine boy, and I wanted to see where he lived."

"But you can't see the boxcar from the hill," said Jessie.

"No, but I came back that night and looked around," said Dr. Moore.

"About ten o'clock!" cried Jessie.

"Yes," said the doctor. "I stepped on a stick, and you heard me."

"Our rabbit!" cried Jessie and Henry. "Watch barked."

"Yes, I heard the dog bark. So I knew you were in the boxcar. Then I went home."

"But you came back?" asked Jessie.

"Oh yes. When you were picking cherries, I went up to see your house. I wanted to see if you had enough to eat and enough dishes."

"Why didn't you tell me?" asked Mr. Alden. "Didn't you know they were my grandchildren?"

The doctor laughed. "Yes, I did. But they were having such a fine time that I didn't want to tell. They got along very well until Violet got sick. Then I told you."

"I'm glad you did," said Mr. Alden.

"I have seen your house too," said Mrs. Moore. "I went up one day and saw all your dishes. I liked your big pitcher and teapot."

"All of you have seen it but me!" said Mr. Alden.

"We'll show it to you!" cried Benny. "I'll show you my

cart made out of wheels, and my pink cup."

"Good for you, Benny," said his grandfather, much pleased. "When Violet gets well, we'll all go up there. If you will show me your house, I'll show you my house."

"Do you have a house?" asked Benny in surprise.

"Yes. You can live there with me if you like it. I have been looking for you children for a long time."

Violet was soon well again, and one afternoon they all started out to see the boxcar. The doctor took them in his car. Many people looked out of their windows to watch Mr. Alden and his grandchildren. They were glad that the children had found such a kind grandfather at last.

When they arrived at their old home, they ran around, all talking excitedly. Watch sniffed and sniffed all around, looking for the bone he had buried. Everything was the same.

"Here is the dam for the pool," said Henry to his grandfather.

"See our 'building'!" shouted Benny, for that was what he called the fireplace. "It really burns too. And this is the refrigerator in the waterfall, and here is my pink cup!"

They all stepped on the stump and climbed into the car. They looked at the four beds and the dishes.

"Here is the same old pitcher and teapot," said Jessie, laughing.

They found the blue tablecloth, and they all sat down by the brook and ate chicken and bread and butter and cookies. Benny drank milk from his pink cup.

"Come, we ought to go now," said Dr. Moore at last. "The sun is going down. I don't want Violet to take any more cold."

They closed the boxcar door and said good-bye. But they were all sorry to go.

"Tomorrow," said Mr. Alden, "will all of you come to see my house?"

"Oh yes," cried the children happily. They did not know what a beautiful house it was and what good times they were going to have in it.

126

Chapter 13

A New Home for the Boxcar

THE CHILDREN'S GRANDFATHER wanted them to like his house. He wanted them to live with him all the time. So he had made over some of the rooms just for them.

The children went with him in his car to see the house. When the car stopped in front of it, Henry cried in surprise, "Do you live *here*, in this beautiful house?"

It was a beautiful house. It was very big, with many trees and flower gardens around it.

"You may live here too, if you like my house," remarked his grandfather, watching Henry's face.

The house was beautiful inside too. There were flowers everywhere. There were maids everywhere. The children went up to the bedrooms.

"Oh!" cried Jessie. "This is Violet's room."

It really was Violet's room. There were violets on the

wallpaper. The bed was white with a violet cover. On the table were flowers.

"What a beautiful room!" cried Violet, sitting down in a soft, pretty chair.

All the children shouted when they saw Benny's room. The wallpaper was blue and covered with big rabbits and dogs and bears. There were a rocking horse and a toolbox and little tables and chairs. And an engine stood on a track, with cars almost as big as the little boy himself. Benny ran over to the engine.

"Can I run this train all day?" he asked. He sat down on the floor by the engine.

"Oh no," said Henry. "You are going to school as soon as it begins."

His grandfather laughed. "That is right, my boy. You will like school. You will learn to read."

"Oh, I can read now," said Benny.

In Jessie's room they found a bed for Watch. It was on the floor by her bed. Watch got in at once, sniffed at the pillow, turned around three times, and lay down.

"He likes it," said Jessie. "He will sleep by me."

Just then the children heard a doorbell ring. A maid came up to find Mr. Alden.

"A man to see you," she said, "about the dog."

Now when Jessie heard the word "dog," she was frightened. She was afraid it was about Watch.

"They won't take Watch away?" she whispered to Henry.

"No, indeed!" said Henry. "We'll never, *never* give him up."

Henry and Jessie and the other children went down with their grandfather to see the man, and Jessie was more frightened than ever. Watch did not growl at the man. He jumped up on him delightedly.

"You see, he was my dog," said the man. "But I sold him to a lady, and he ran away from her that very day. I have to turn him over to the lady I sold him to."

"How do you know he is the same dog?" asked Mr. Alden.

"Oh, he is my dog," said the man. "You see he knows

me, and he has a small black spot on this foot. But someone has cut his hair on one side."

Benny looked. He found the black spot on Watch's foot.

"I never saw that spot before," said Henry.

"I will give you what you want for the dog," said Mr. Alden. "The children love him. They want to keep him."

"But I sold him to a lady," said the man. "I must take the dog to her."

Then Henry said, "Maybe she will want to change to another dog when she sees his hair. If she will agree to take another dog, will you let my grandfather have this one?"

"Yes, I will," said the man.

"Let's go and ask her, Grandfather," said Benny. "She will let Jessie have Watch. He is her dog. She took the thorn out of his foot."

The man told Mr. Alden where the lady lived, and they all started out to find her. She was a very pretty young lady, and she asked them to sit down.

But Benny could not wait. He said, "Please let us keep Watch! I want him, and Jessie wants him, and we didn't know he was your dog."

"What do you mean?" asked the lady, laughing. "Who is Watch?"

"This dog is Watch," answered Henry. "A man came to Grandfather's house today and told us that he had sold the dog to you. When Watch ran away from you, the day you bought him, he came to us. He had a thorn in his foot, and Jessie took it out."

Watch looked up at the lady and wagged his tail. When she looked at him, she began to laugh.

"Look at his side!" she said. "Who cut his hair?"

"I'm sorry," said Henry. "Benny did that one day with Violet's scissors."

"I am not sorry," said the lady, laughing. "He looks so funny. And you want to keep him? Is that it?"

"Oh yes," said Jessie eagerly. "The man will let us have him, if you will take another dog."

"Don't be afraid," said the young lady. "You may keep the dog. I can change to another one."

"Oh, thank you! You are nice!" cried Benny.

He ran to the lady and climbed up in her lap before anyone could stop him.

"I'd like to keep you, Benny, in place of the dog," laughed the lady, putting her arms around him.

How happy the children were to have Watch to keep! Mr. Alden gave the money to the man at once.

Four happy children sat with their grandfather around the Alden dinner table that night. The maids smiled in the kitchen to hear the children laugh. And the children laughed because Watch had a chair at the table beside Jessie and was really waited on by a maid.

Would you ever think that four children could be homesick in such a beautiful house? Jessie was the first one to wish for the old boxcar.

One day she said, "Oh, Grandfather, I'd like to cook something once more in the dear old kettle in the woods."

"Go out in the kitchen, my dear," said her grandfather. "The maids will help you. You can cook all you want to."

Jessie liked this, but it was not like the old days in the boxcar.

132

Then one day Benny said, "Grandfather, I wish I could drink my milk out of my dear old pink cup."

His grandfather began to think. He had some pink cups, but they were not so dear to Benny as his old cracked one.

At last Mr. Alden said, "I am going to give you children a surprise."

"Is it very nice?" asked Benny.

"No, not very," laughed his grandfather. "It is not pretty at all."

"When will it come?" asked Benny.

"It will come today. You children must all go over to Dr. Moore's and stay, until the surprise comes."

"What can it be?" wondered Violet.

Her grandfather laughed. "I hope you will like it," he said. "It is very heavy."

The children were glad to see sweet Mrs. Moore and the kind doctor again. They stayed until Mr. Alden said the surprise was ready. Then Dr. Moore and his mother went back with them in the big car.

Mr. Alden was as happy as a boy. He took them by the garage and through the big gardens. At last they came to a garden with a fountain in the middle and trees around it. Near the fountain was the surprise. It was the old boxcar!

The children ran over to it with cries of delight, opened the door, and climbed in. All the things were in place. Even the old dead stump was there to step on.

Here was the old knife which had cut butter and bread and vegetables and firewood and string. Here was Benny's pink cup, and here was his bed. Here were the big kettle and the blue tablecloth. Here were the pitcher and the old teapot. And here was the dinner bell, which the children had made from an old tin can.

Benny hung it on a tree with a string and rang it over and over again with a spoon. Watch rolled on the floor of the car and barked and barked. Then he began to sniff at everything.

"He's looking for the bone he buried," laughed Benny.

"How they love the old boxcar!" said Mrs. Moore. "I like to see them so happy."

"Thank you for the surprise, Grandfather," said Violet. "We'll never go away from you again."

"I hope not, my dear," said Mr. Alden. "We'll all live happily ever after."

And so they did.

A Story with Many Beginnings

Gertrude Chandler Warner and the Making of *The Boxcar Children*

While this edition of *The Boxcar Children* celebrates the seventy-fifth anniversary of its release, the history of this beloved classic goes back long before its publication in 1942, starting with the childhood of its author, Gertrude Chandler Warner, and continuing through decades of discovery, development, writing, and revision.

Warner was born on April 16, 1890, in Putnam, Connecticut. Her family had deep New England roots, and she grew up in a house built by her grandfather near the railroad tracks. At the time, Putnam was an important railway hub connecting several rail lines. "I used to watch the

▲ *Gertrude Chandler Warner, two years old, with her older sister, Frances*

◄ *Cover of* Short Stories, *a book Gertrude Chandler Warner made for her grandmother for Christmas in 1901, featuring a photograph of eleven-year-old Gertrude*

▲ *The Warner family when Gertrude Chandler Warner was five years old. From left to right: Edgar, John (seated in his father's lap), Frances, Gertrude, and Jennie.*

long freight trains going by, each with a caboose on the end," Warner recalled in a 1938 magazine article. Trains bound for New York and Boston passed by many times a day. She especially loved looking through caboose windows to glimpse the living spaces inside. "I could see the men sitting at a table eating by the light of a lantern," she recalled. "This sight always made me want to play house in a

▼ *Landscape, with train, from a book Warner made when she was about five years old*

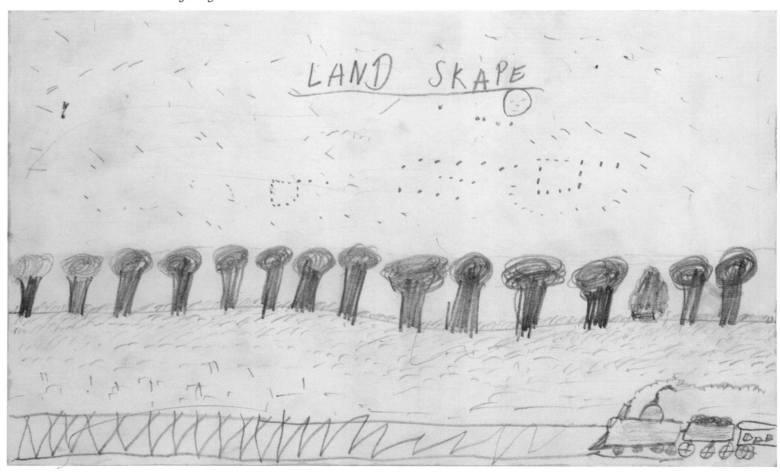

LAND SKAPE

caboose." It was Warner's earliest inspiration for the story that would become *The Boxcar Children.*

In her youth, Warner was a voracious reader and was drawn to writing, art, and music. She played cello, and wrote and illustrated handmade books, which she gave to her grandparents every Christmas. But she was prone to frequent illness as well—sore throats and respiratory problems that forced her to leave high school in her second year and study at home with a tutor. Warner continued her education but never graduated. As her older sister, Frances, and her younger brother, John, left home to attend college, she turned to writing as a vocation. At first she contributed to a local Sunday school newspaper. Then in 1916 she published her first book, *The House of Delight*, a story about her childhood dollhouse and doll collection. Only a thousand copies

▲ *The Warners. Standing: Gertrude (age eleven), Frances, and John. Seated: Edgar and Jennie.*

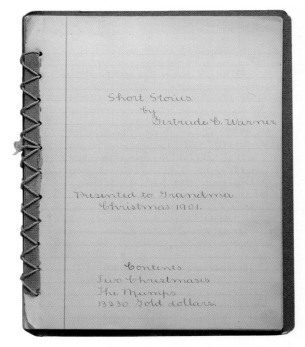

▲ *Title page of* Short Stories, *a book Warner gave to her grandmother. Contents: "Two Christmases," "The Mumps," and "13230 Gold Dollars."*

◄ *Cover for* The House of Delight, *Gertrude Chandler Warner's first book*

were printed, but this first publication was thrilling to twenty-six-year-old Warner. "It was an epoch," she said.

When the United States entered World War I the following year, Warner was publishing stories and essays in magazines and doing publicity work for the Red Cross. But another career opportunity presented itself when war enlistment created a shortage of schoolteachers. In 1918 she became a teaching assistant for the first grade at the Israel Putnam School in her hometown. Warner thought the position would be temporary, but when the instructor she was assisting became a victim of

" WILL YOU HAVE ALICE-BLUE SUITS TRIMMED WITH WHITE BRAID ? "

◄ *Interior photograph from* The House of Delight

the influenza epidemic that year, Warner took over as a full-time teacher. She didn't have a high school diploma, but she learned quickly on the job, teaching both a morning and an afternoon class—a total of eighty children. She went on to stay at Israel Putnam School for more than three decades, teaching first and third grade, and treating students with empathy and respect. She once said the children in her classes were "beneath me only in years."

▲ *Israel Putnam School, where Gertrude Chandler Warner taught first grade and third grade*

▼ *Warner and her first grade students at Israel Putnam School, 1924*

MARCH 1922   THE CURTIS PUBLISHING COMPANY PHILADELPHIA   15 CENTS

Beginning FOURSQUARE: *By* Grace S. Richmond

LIFE'S MINOR COLLISIONS

BY

FRANCES AND GERTRUDE WARNER

AUTHORS (RESPECTIVELY) OF " ENDICOTT AND I "
AND " HOUSE OF DELIGHT "

BOSTON AND NEW YORK
HOUGHTON MIFFLIN COMPANY
The Riverside Press Cambridge
1921

While she taught, Warner continued to write in her spare time. She and her sister, Frances, collaborated on lighthearted essays that were published in magazines like *Ladies' Home Journal* and the *Atlantic Monthly*; many of the articles were collected into a 1921 book for adults called *Life's Minor Collisions*. On her own, Warner wrote for children, including stories for *Little Folks* magazine and a book about constellations, and she occasionally did freelance writing for religious organizations as well. Her health was still fragile, and though she sometimes had to stay home from her teaching job due to illness, she took advantage of these times of "enforced leisure" (as she called it) to focus on her writing.

It was on one such break that Warner was inspired to write the story that would eventually become *The Boxcar Children*. She had recently finished an extensive

Title page for Life's Minor Collisions

write-to-order project and wanted to do something different. "I decided to write a book just to suit myself," she said. She remembered her childhood fascination with living in a train car. She found a blank notebook and pencils. "All wrapped up in quilts...before an open fireplace, I started to write the story," she recalled later. She imagined four orphaned siblings finding an old boxcar in the woods.

▲ *Railroad boxcar, 1900. Train cars like these fascinated Gertrude Chandler Warner when she was a child.*

According to Warner, she was so caught up in the plot that before she knew it, it was noon, and she had just finished the scene in which the four children take shelter in the boxcar during a rainstorm. The substitute teacher for Warner's class stopped by on her lunch break and read the pages. The woman was so intrigued that she visited again after school to read more.

▲ *Gertrude Chandler Warner, circa 1930s*

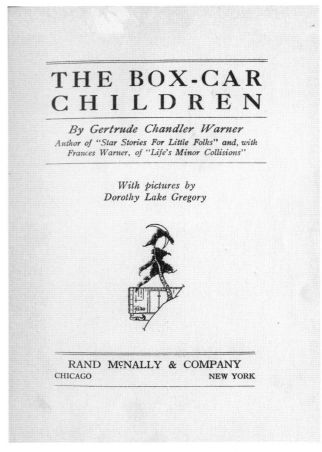

▲ *Title page of* The Box-Car Children

"So really I kept on writing because I knew that twice each day she was coming in to see what 'my children' had done," Warner said. "In this way the whole book was finished before I was able to go back to school. But long before that, the four children had become real children to me."

In 1924 Rand McNally published Warner's manuscript with accompanying illustrations from Dorothy Lake Gregory. The novel was called *The Box-Car Children*, and although the plot is somewhat similar to *The Boxcar Children*—which Warner wrote much later—this little-known precursor is a significantly different work: longer, more slowly paced, and written for an advanced reading level. In this earlier book, the four central characters, siblings Henry, Jess, Violet, and Benny, went by the last name Cordyce instead of Alden; Henry worked for a Dr. McAllister instead of Dr. Moore; and Benny's homemade

▶ *Front cover illustration by Dorothy Lake Gregory for* The Box-Car Children, *depicting Jess and Benny Cordyce*

THE BOX-CAR CHILDREN

GERTRUDE C. WARNER

Henry felt himself lifted on many shoulders

▲ *Color plate from* The Box-Car Children. *Illustration by Dorothy Lake Gregory.*

stuffed bear was named Ginseng, not Stockings. The version of the story that generations of readers know and love was not written for several more years.

Not much is known about the critical reception of the 1924 book. *The Box-Car Children* was published at a time when few publications reviewed children's books. Warner, however, recounted her own experiences years later, saying that the book "raised a storm of protest from librarians, who thought the children were having too good a time without any parental control!" She noted slyly, "That is exactly why children like it!"

Despite its appealing premise, the

The Box-Car Children was out of print by the 1930s, when the children's book market was severely curtailed by the Great Depression. Today, copies of the book are extremely rare and collectible.

While Warner kept writing, publishing, and teaching through the Depression years, a car accident in 1932 left her with a broken back, requiring a lengthy hospital stay and several months of recovery

▼ *Warner and her sister, Frances, in 1933*

25 CENTS

N.S.E.

MARCH 1938

CHILD LIFE

The Children's Own Magazine

CLARENCE BIERS

time. Nonetheless she forced herself to finish a book she was working on with her sister. She later spoke of this time, saying "You can do a lot of things you think you can't." Through these years of persistence, the story she had written years before—about four children living in a boxcar, determined to make a home for themselves together—seemed to stay with her, for she would return to it more than once over the next decade.

By the late 1930s, Warner was well enough to travel and spend her summer vacation time teaching courses at Yale University. In 1938 she published another version of her boxcar story, this time as an eight-part serial in *Child Life* magazine called "The Box-Car Adventure." The first installment, accompanied by illustrations by Marguerite Davis, ran

▲ *Paper dolls to accompany "The Box-Car Adventure" serial in* Child Life *magazine, 1938*

► *Illustration by Marguerite Davis for the first installment of the serial "The Box-Car Adventure"*

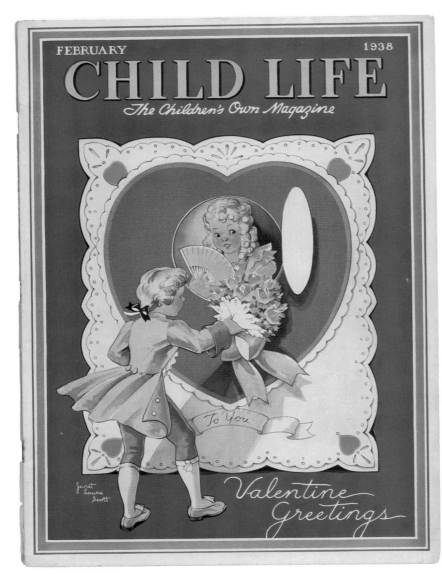

▲ *One of the issues of* Child Life *magazine in which the serial "The Box-Car Adventure" appeared*

in the February 1938 issue and continued for seven more months. The opening scene of the story had changed since the 1924 book: in this new version, the four orphaned siblings stood in front of a bakery one warm evening. Their names had changed as well—they were now known as Henry, Jess, Violet, and Benny Alden. "The Box-Car Adventure" still had much in common with the older book, *The Box-Car Children*, but it was clear that Warner's idea was evolving as she edited scenes, revised details, and renamed characters and places.

A few years later, Warner took a summer job in Chicago as an educational consultant for Scott, Foresman and

Company. A salesman for the textbook publisher had visited her classroom at Israel Putnam School to sell her the company's line of Elson Readers, the series in which the *Dick and Jane* stories first appeared. When the salesman learned that Warner wrote children's books, he put her in touch with the company's editorial staff, who offered her a job developing stories for beginning readers.

Warner's job was to find material for older children who were still learning to read independently but needed more engaging stories to hold their interest. She searched bookstores for exciting stories that she could rewrite with simpler language; at some point she realized that her own book was an ideal choice. Warner had been reading *The Box-Car Children* to her students for years, after all, and sometimes had them read passages back to her. Not only did she know which parts of the

▲ *Primer from the Elson Readers series, which Warner taught in her classroom*

▲ *The YWCA residence in Chicago where Warner worked on* The Boxcar Children

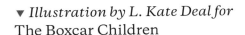

▼ *Illustration by L. Kate Deal for* The Boxcar Children

story the children in her classes enjoyed, she also knew the kinds of words and sentences they struggled with most.

So Warner returned, once more, to the story about the brothers and sisters living in a boxcar. She wrote in her room at the YWCA McCormick Memorial Residence for Women at Oak and Dearborn Streets in Chicago. By Warner's own account, it was a hot summer, with consecutive days of temperatures higher than 100 degrees (weather records indicate this may have been in July 1940), but she said, "I like hot weather and had a grand time." She loved that she was earning a salary to write.

Her work involved considerable revision of her original story. She simplified and limited the vocabulary so that the narrative used a list of only 600 words that were easy for beginning readers to decode. She trimmed the novel down to 15,000 words total, doing away with the lengthy descriptions that had frustrated her students. The resulting story retained all the essential action of the 1924 novel, but now a much wider audience could follow along—reluctant readers, readers learning English, readers eager to read independently and build their confidence—all savoring the adventures of four children who were themselves experiencing the world on their own for the first time.

This final version was called *The Boxcar Children*, and it has endured. Published and copyrighted in 1942 by Scott, Foresman and Company, the book was illustrated by L. Kate Deal, a Louisiana-born artist who worked in Chicago. Deal frequently did artwork for educational publications, including the Elson Readers, and the ink silhouette

▲ *Illustration by L. Kate Deal for* The Boxcar Children

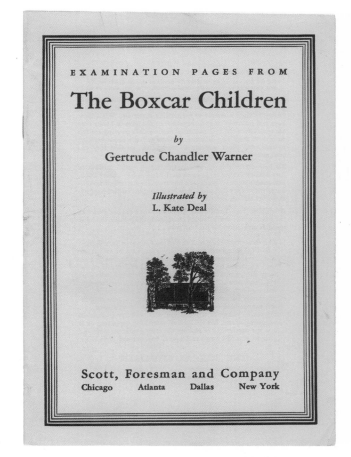

▲ *Exam booklet for* The Boxcar Children

155

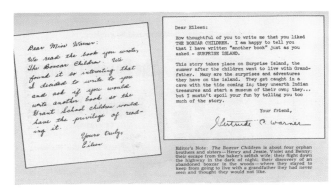

▲ *Promotional materials from Scott, Foresman and Company, circa 1949*

artwork she created for *The Boxcar Children* became one of its most iconic features. The book was immediately popular with teachers and students and soon went into new printings—an unusual success in the World War II years when paper rationing was in effect. Young readers wrote to Warner, and she called these letters her "prop and stay." One of her favorites read (with a couple small spelling mistakes): "I like *The Boxcar Children* because the children seeck there own life."

In response to the popularity of the first book and requests from children for more adventures about the Aldens, Warner wrote a sequel, *Surprise Island*, in 1949. The letters from readers continued, and by

▼ *Promotional materials from Scott, Foresman and Company*

the 1950s the Boxcar Children had become a mystery series. Though the books were distributed through schools as part of a third-grade reading curriculum, children wanted their own copies to read at home, so Scott, Foresman partnered with another Chicago publisher, Albert Whitman & Company, to produce trade editions of the Boxcar Children books to be sold to bookstores and the public.

Warner's working relationship with Albert Whitman and Company would last the rest of her life. In the 1960s, Albert Whitman acquired the full rights for *The Boxcar Children* and became the primary publisher of all its sequels. Editor Caroline Rubin worked with Warner as she continued the adventures of the Alden family for a total of nineteen books, publishing the last one, *Benny Uncovers a Mystery*, in 1976. Warner passed away three years

▲ 1964 newspaper ad for Mountain Top Mystery *in Putnam, Connecticut, Gertrude Chandler Warner's hometown*

WINDHAM COUNTY OBSERVER — PUTNAM PATRIOT
Wednesday, December 2, 1964   Putnam, Connecticut   **13**

Publishers Bring Out New Warner Book

Miss Gertrude C. Warner's tremendously popular stories of the Boxcar Children will continue.

The publishers have just announced the issuance of a new book about the children called "The Mountain Top Mystery." Children are certain to receive this book with enthusiasm as all these books are very easy reading with high interest content.

The publishers state that the story starts out with a simple, one-day mountain-climb with "Gramps" as leader. However, like all these stories, there are many unforeseen complications which make this one of the most exciting books of the series of nine. Miss Warner has an order for the tenth book.

Miss Warner, author of these books, is a former local teacher and has twenty or more books to her credit. She is listed in "Who's Who in America."

This new mystery, in addition to all the other Boxcar books, is on sale at Shaw's Stationers in Putnam.

GERTRUDE C. WARNER
(Photo by Grube)

▲ A 1964 article about Gertrude Chandler Warner in the Windham County Observer— Putnam Patriot

▶ *Page 158: First edition of* The Boxcar Children

▶ *Page 159: First editions of the second, third, fourth, and fifth books in the Boxcar Children series:* Surprise Island, The Yellow House Mystery, Mystery Ranch, *and* Mike's Mystery

The Boxcar
Children

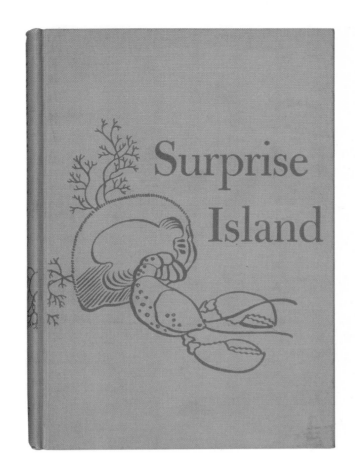

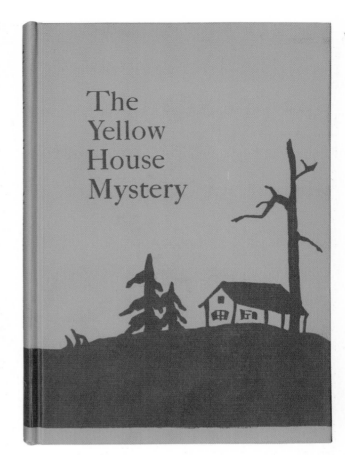

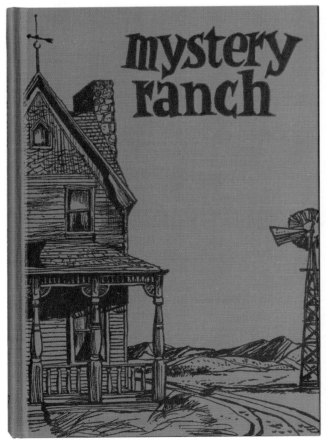

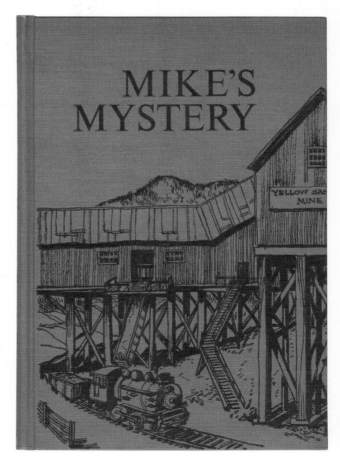

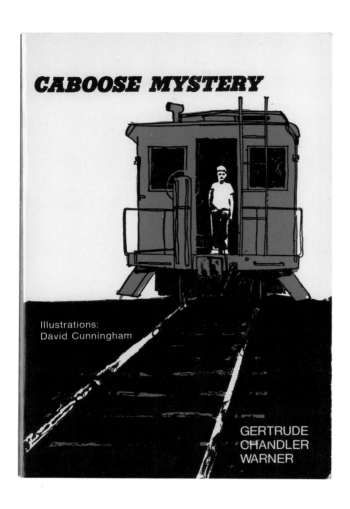

later, in Putnam, at the age of eighty-nine, after a long illness.

In the more than thirty years following Warner's death, *The Boxcar Children* has remained in print. It has been translated into six languages, adapted as a successful children's play, and made into an acclaimed animated feature. Letters from children still come to the Albert Whitman offices on a regular basis.

At its heart, *The Boxcar Children* is a story about empathy, resourcefulness, and reconsideration. When the Aldens meet their grandfather and realize how much he loves them, they put aside their old fears and beliefs about him to begin a new life as a family. In much the same way, Gertrude Chandler Warner used her insights as a writer and teacher to better understand her readers and see an old story in a new light. More than seven decades later, that light still shines. ∎

▲ *In her own hand, Gertrude Chandler Warner's dedication for* The Woodshed Mystery, *the seventh book in the Boxcar Children series: "To all readers everywhere, including Guam, who have written to me about the Boxcar Children, this new mystery is dedicated."*

▼ *Gertrude Chandler Warner, while researching* Caboose Mystery. *"I myself took a trip by caboose, riding on the back platform and feeling just like Benny."*

MISS GERTRUDE C. WARNER
22 RING STREET
PUTNAM, CONNECTICUT 06260

Dear Friend,

I do appreciate your kind letter about the Boxcar Children books. I am sorry not to write a longer letter, but I am very busy writing another book about the Aldens.

If you read the enclosed material, some of your questions will be answered. Yes, it is true that I started to write when I was able to hold a pencil. These stories were not published. I write one book every year.

The first thing I do when I am starting to write a book is get a notebook to write in. That way the story is all in one place. I always put down notes in this book and pieces of conversation. I also get one dozen soft pencils all sharpened. When a pencil gets hot and "tired" I change to a new one.

If you are interested in writing, never throw away what you write. You may want it later.

Good luck to you.

Your sincere friend,
Gertrude C. Warner

▲ *1960s letter from Warner sent as response to fan mail*

▶ *Page 162: Illustration by L. Kate Deal for* The Boxcar Children

Sources

Abate, Michelle Ann. "*The Boxcar Children* and *The Box-Car Children*: The Rewriting of Gertrude Chandler Warner's Classic and the Origins of the Early Reader." In *The Early Reader in Children's Literature and Culture: Theorizing Books for Beginning Readers*, edited by Jennifer Miskec and Annette Wannamaker, 26-37. New York: Routledge, 2016.

Ellsworth, Mary Ellen. *Gertrude Chandler Warner and the Boxcar Children*. Morton Grove, IL: Albert Whitman & Company, 1997.

"Three Toots and a Whistle for Gertrude Chandler Warner!!!" *The Score*, April 1967: 4-5.

Warner, Gertrude Chandler. "The Editor's Mailbag: A Letter from Gertrude Chandler Warner." *Child Life*, June 1938: 288.

Photo and Image Credits